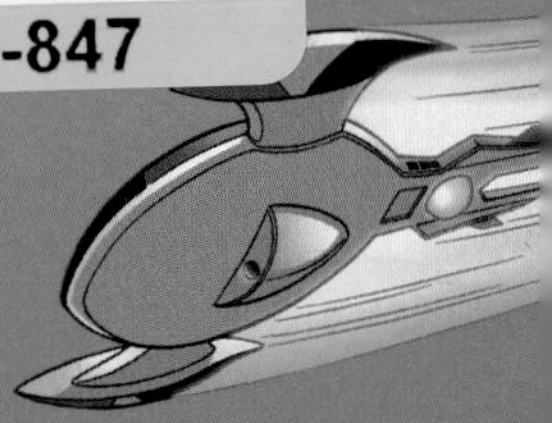

GREEN LANTERN

THE ANIMATED SERIES™

GOLDFACE ATTACKS!

Art Baltazar & Franco....................writers
Dario Brizuela............................illustrator
Saida Temofonte ....letterer

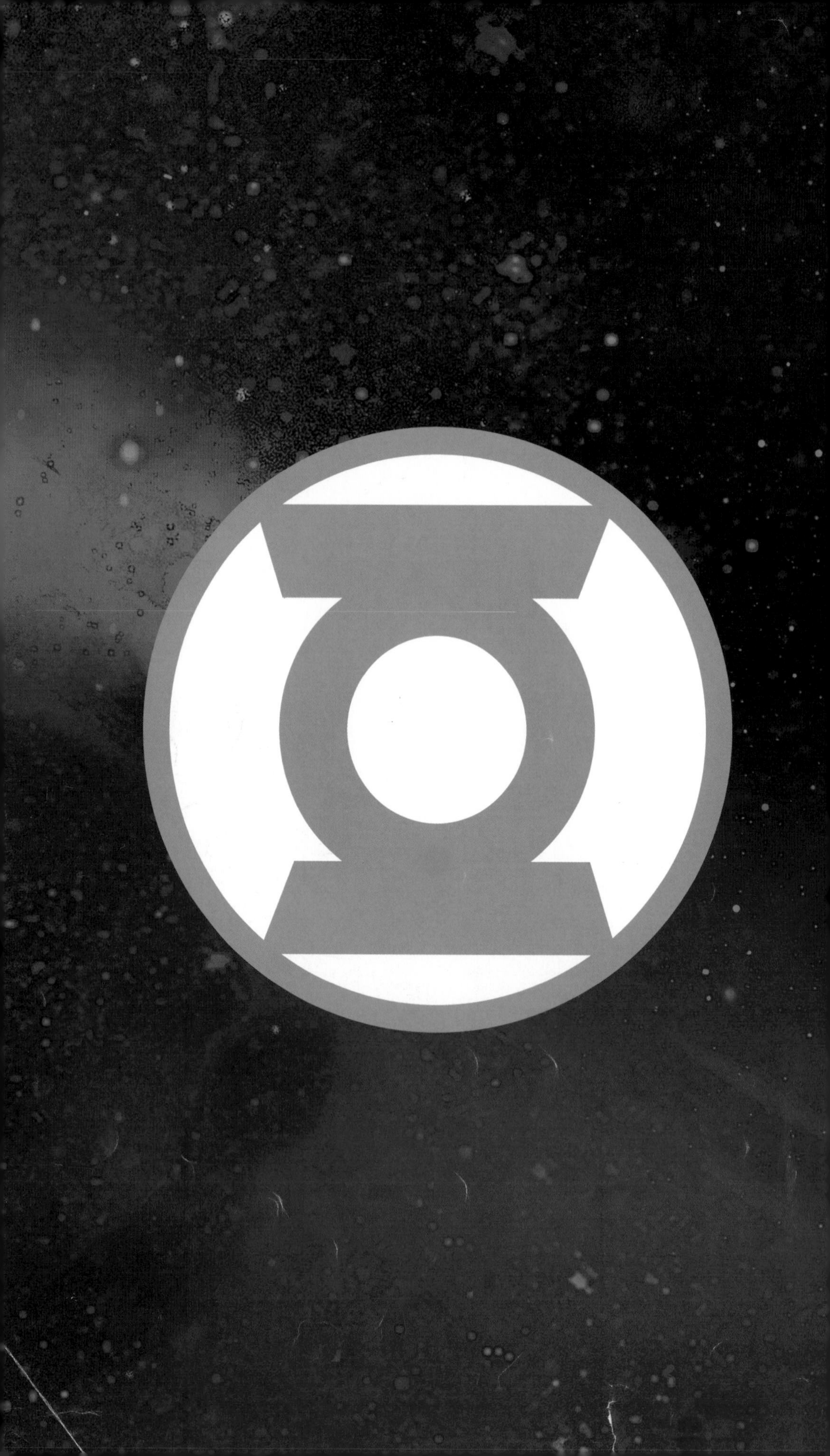

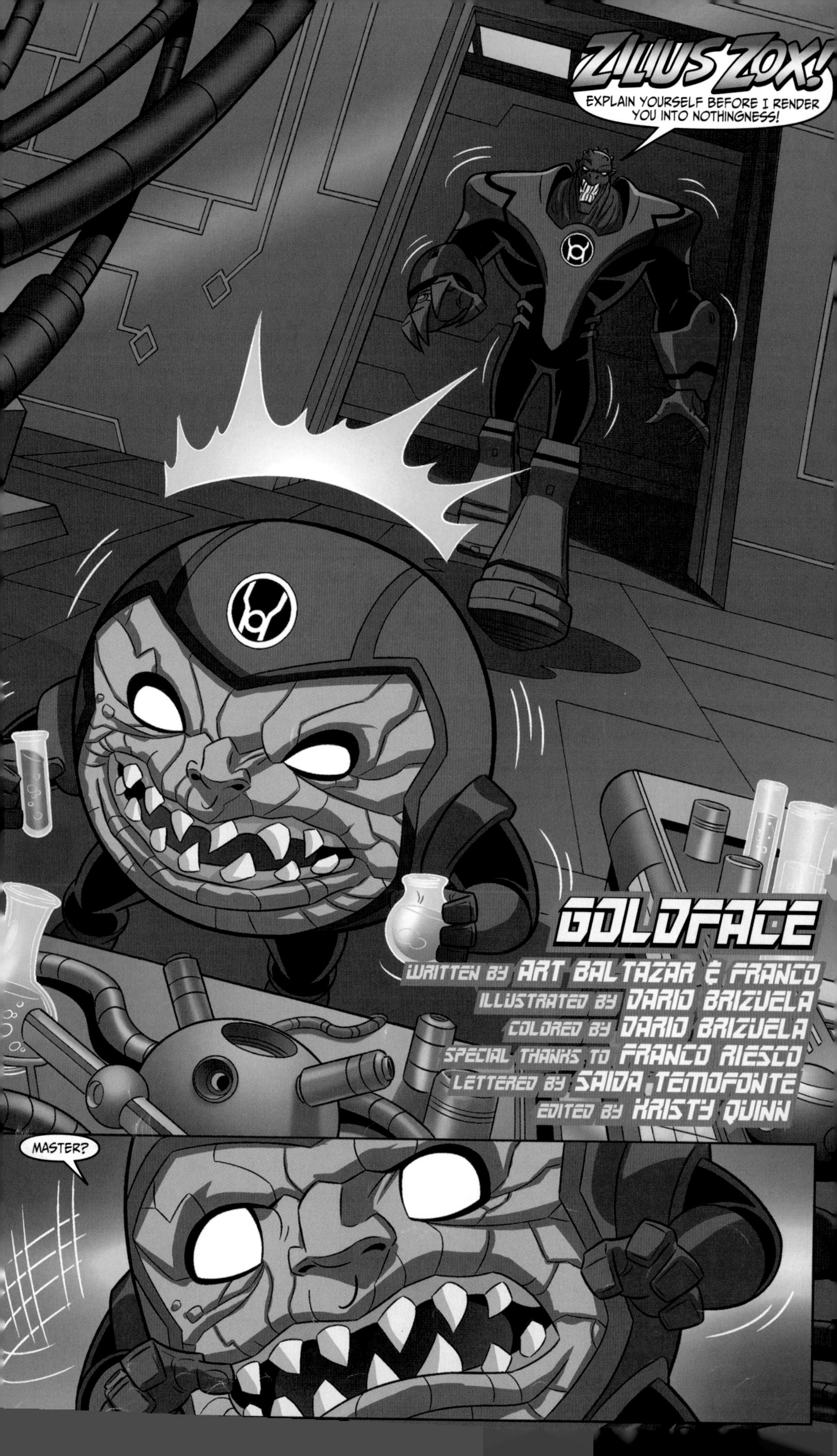
ZILIUS ZOX!
EXPLAIN YOURSELF BEFORE I RENDER YOU INTO NOTHINGNESS!
GOLDFACE
WRITTEN BY ART BALTAZAR & FRANCO
ILLUSTRATED BY DARIO BRIZUELA
COLORED BY DARIO BRIZUELA
SPECIAL THANKS TO FRANCO RIESCO
LETTERED BY SAIDA TEMOFONTE
EDITED BY KRISTY QUINN
MASTER?

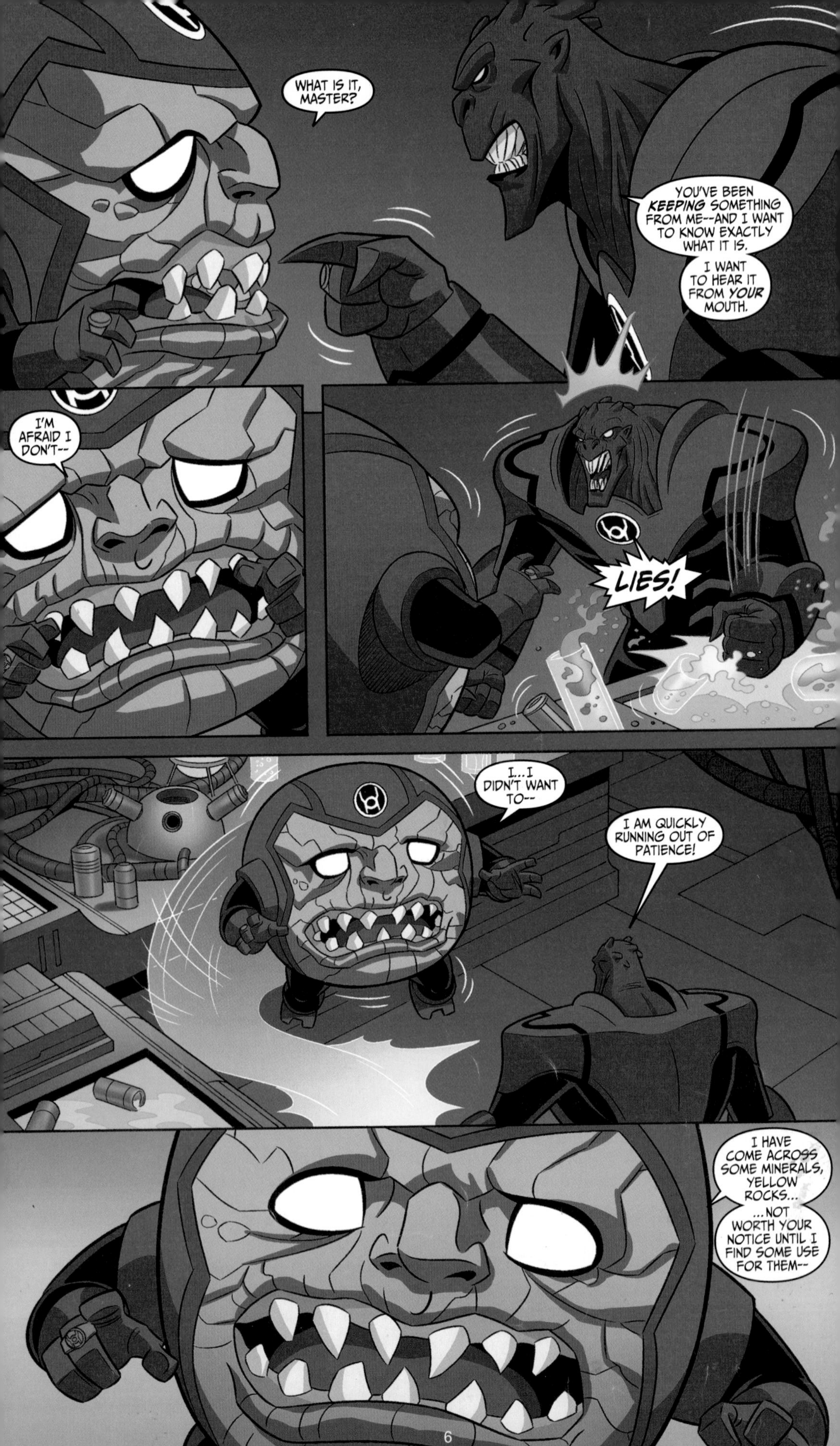
WHAT IS IT, MASTER?
YOU'VE BEEN KEEPING SOMETHING FROM ME--AND I WANT TO KNOW EXACTLY WHAT IT IS.
I WANT TO HEAR IT FROM YOUR MOUTH.
I'M AFRAID I DON'T--
LIES!
I...I DIDN'T WANT TO--
I AM QUICKLY RUNNING OUT OF PATIENCE!
I HAVE COME ACROSS SOME MINERALS, YELLOW ROCKS...
...NOT WORTH YOUR NOTICE UNTIL I FIND SOME USE FOR THEM--

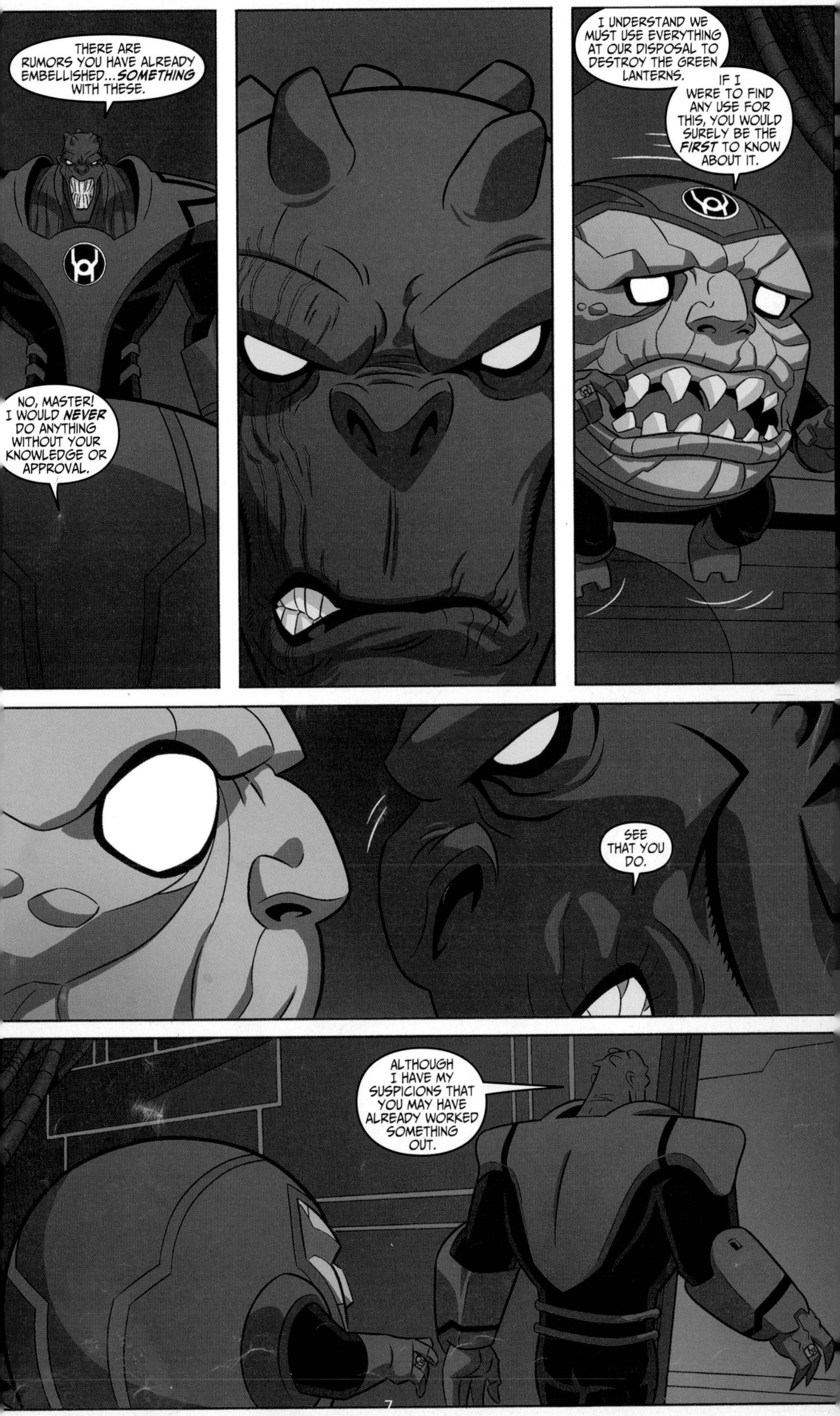
THERE ARE RUMORS YOU HAVE ALREADY EMBELLISHED...SOMETHING WITH THESE.
NO, MASTER! I WOULD NEVER DO ANYTHING WITHOUT YOUR KNOWLEDGE OR APPROVAL.
I UNDERSTAND WE MUST USE EVERYTHING AT OUR DISPOSAL TO DESTROY THE GREEN LANTERNS.
IF I WERE TO FIND ANY USE FOR THIS, YOU WOULD SURELY BE THE FIRST TO KNOW ABOUT IT.
SEE THAT YOU DO.
ALTHOUGH I HAVE MY SUSPICIONS THAT YOU MAY HAVE ALREADY WORKED SOMETHING OUT.

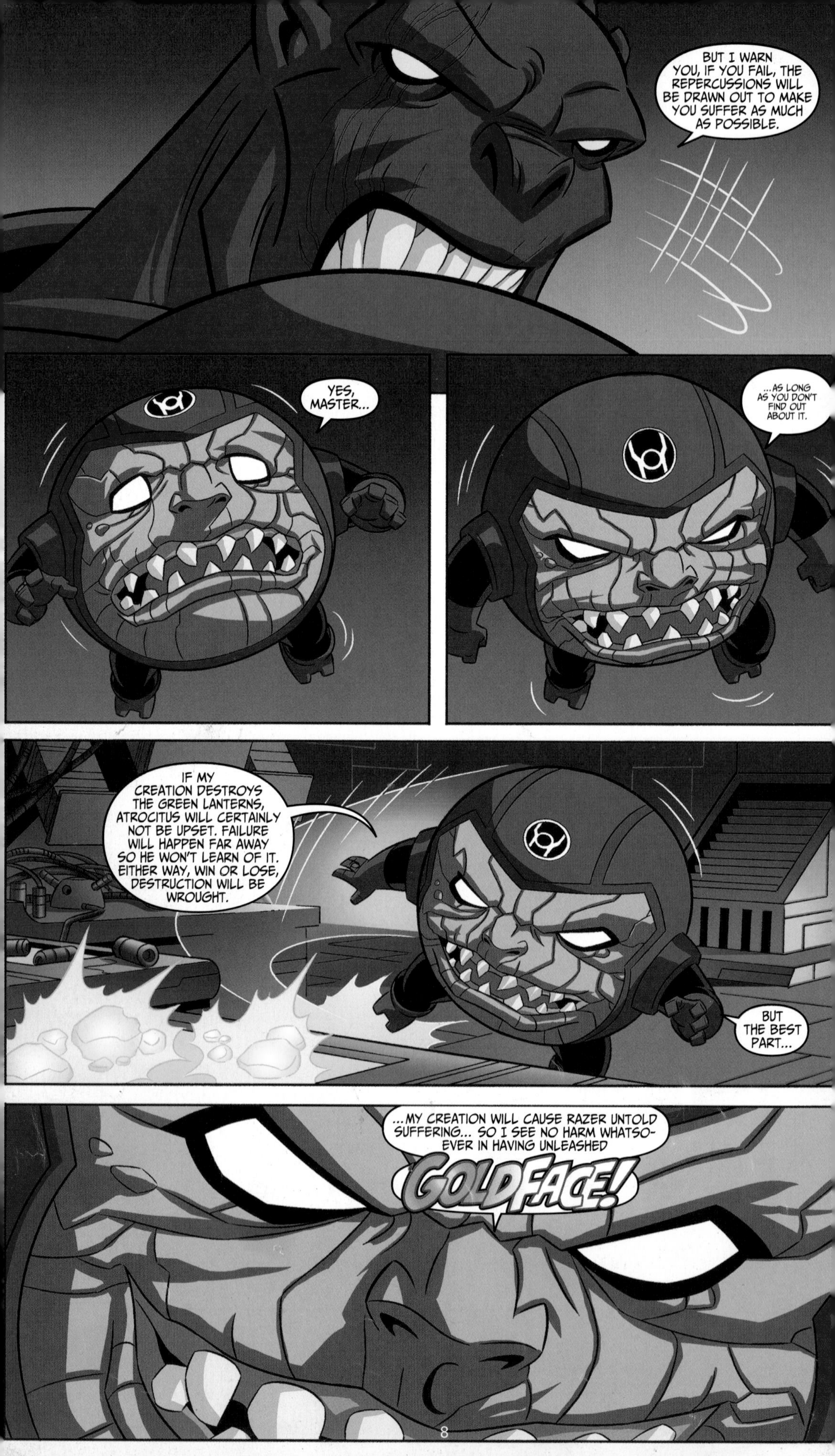
BUT I WARN YOU, IF YOU FAIL, THE REPERCUSSIONS WILL BE DRAWN OUT TO MAKE YOU SUFFER AS MUCH AS POSSIBLE.
YES, MASTER...
...AS LONG AS YOU DON'T FIND OUT ABOUT IT.
IF MY CREATION DESTROYS THE GREEN LANTERNS, ATROCITUS WILL CERTAINLY NOT BE UPSET. FAILURE WILL HAPPEN FAR AWAY SO HE WON'T LEARN OF IT. EITHER WAY, WIN OR LOSE, DESTRUCTION WILL BE WROUGHT.
BUT THE BEST PART...
...MY CREATION WILL CAUSE RAZER UNTOLD SUFFERING... SO I SEE NO HARM WHATSO- EVER IN HAVING UNLEASHED
GOLDFACE!

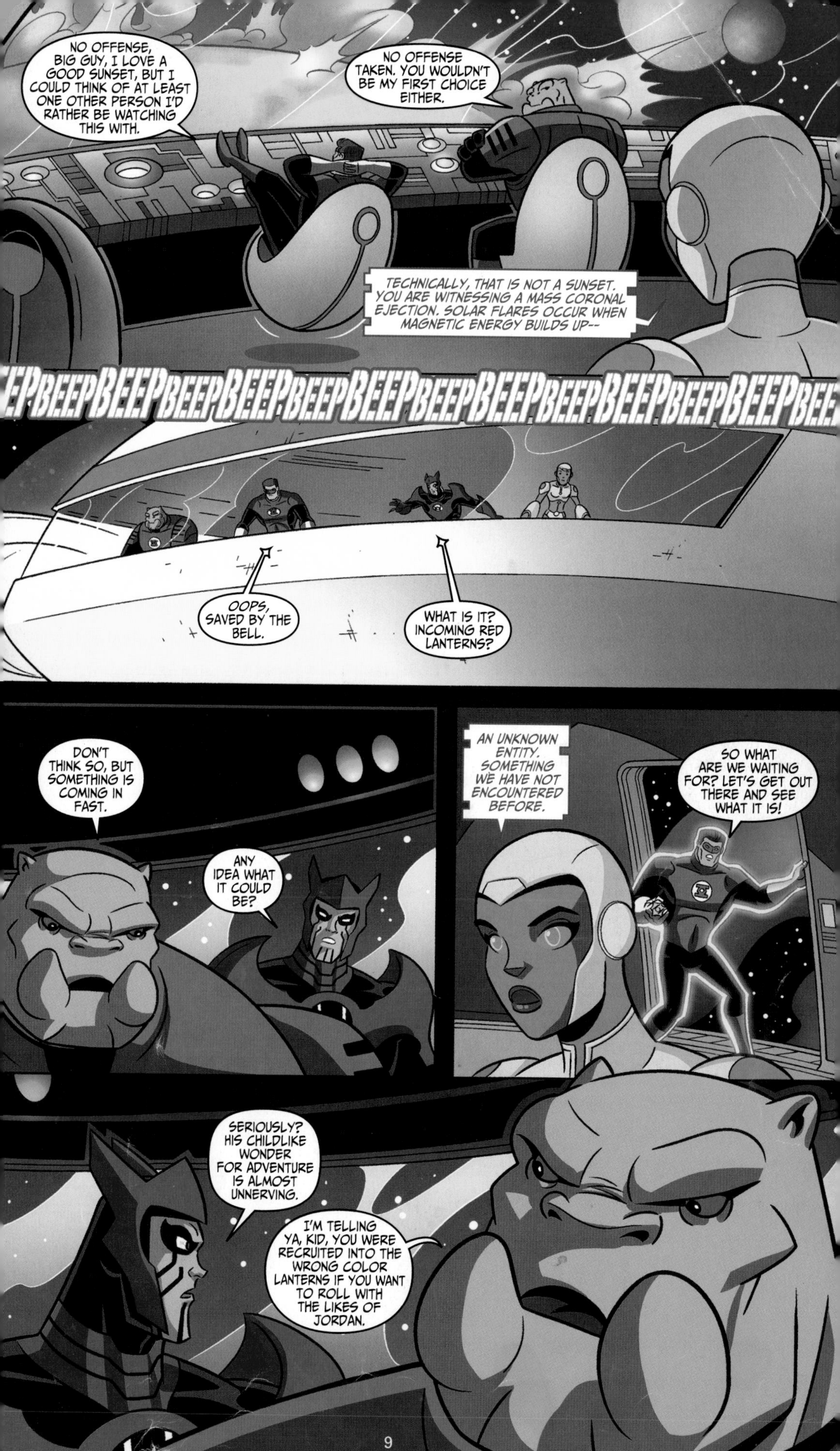
NO OFFENSE, BIG GUY, I LOVE A GOOD SUNSET, BUT I COULD THINK OF AT LEAST ONE OTHER PERSON I'D RATHER BE WATCHING THIS WITH.
NO OFFENSE TAKEN. YOU WOULDN'T BE MY FIRST CHOICE EITHER.
TECHNICALLY, THAT IS NOT A SUNSET. YOU ARE WITNESSING A MASS CORONAL EJECTION. SOLAR FLARES OCCUR WHEN MAGNETIC ENERGY BUILDS UP--
EPBEEPBEEPBEEPBEEPBEEPBEEPBEEPBEEPBEEPBEEPBEEPBEEPBEE
OOPS, SAVED BY THE BELL.
WHAT IS IT? INCOMING RED LANTERNS?
DON'T THINK SO, BUT SOMETHING IS COMING IN FAST.
ANY IDEA WHAT IT COULD BE?
AN UNKNOWN ENTITY. SOMETHING WE HAVE NOT ENCOUNTERED BEFORE.
SO WHAT ARE WE WAITING FOR? LET'S GET OUT THERE AND SEE WHAT IT IS!
SERIOUSLY? HIS CHILDLIKE WONDER FOR ADVENTURE IS ALMOST UNNERVING.
I'M TELLING YA, KID, YOU WERE RECRUITED INTO THE WRONG COLOR LANTERNS IF YOU WANT TO ROLL WITH THE LIKES OF JORDAN.

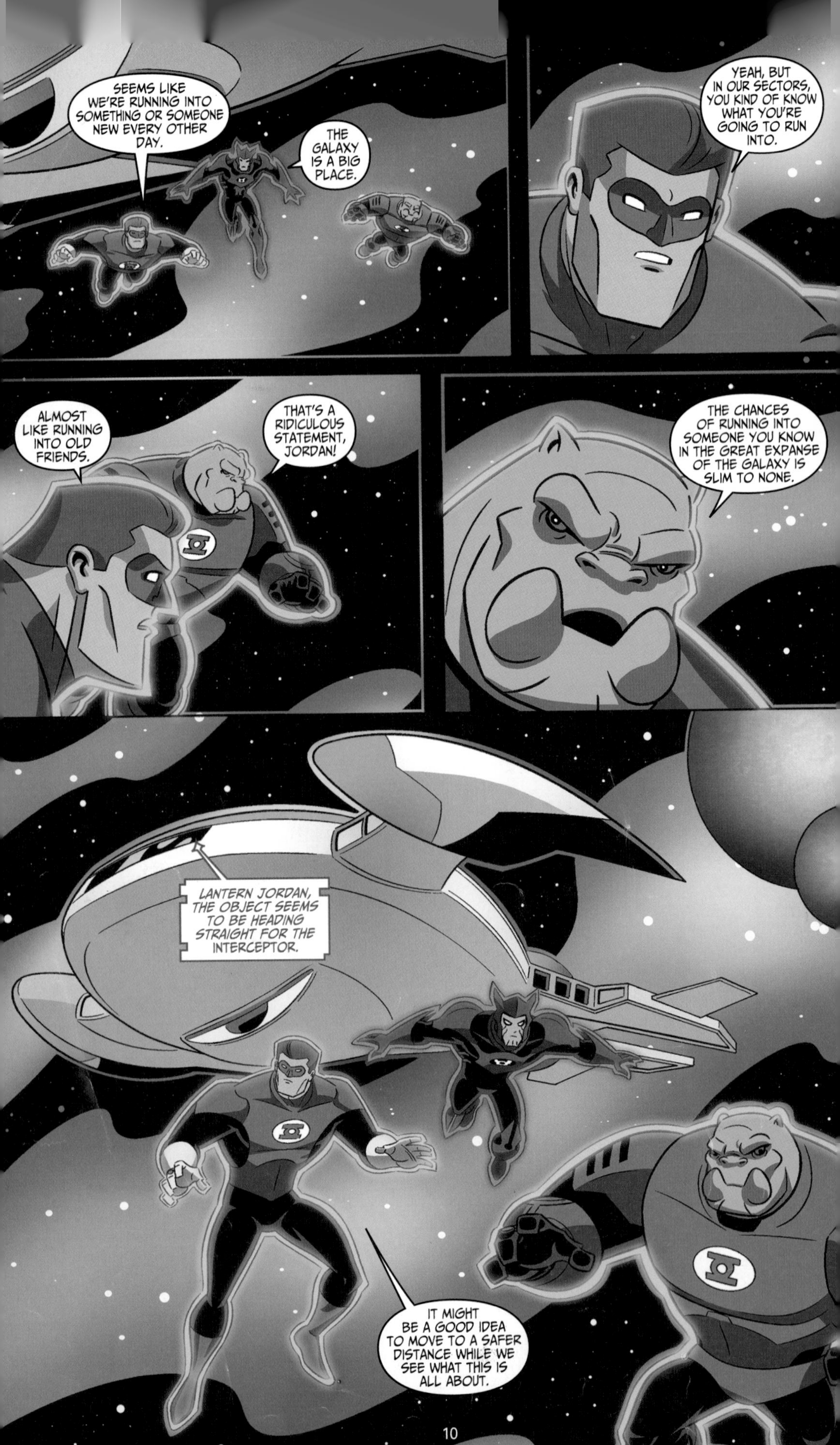

SEEMS LIKE WE'RE RUNNING INTO SOMETHING OR SOMEONE NEW EVERY OTHER DAY.
THE GALAXY IS A BIG PLACE.
YEAH, BUT IN OUR SECTORS, YOU KIND OF KNOW WHAT YOU'RE GOING TO RUN INTO.
ALMOST LIKE RUNNING INTO OLD FRIENDS.
THAT'S A RIDICULOUS STATEMENT, JORDAN!
THE CHANCES OF RUNNING INTO SOMEONE YOU KNOW IN THE GREAT EXPANSE OF THE GALAXY IS SLIM TO NONE.
LANTERN JORDAN, THE OBJECT SEEMS TO BE HEADING STRAIGHT FOR THE INTERCEPTOR.
IT MIGHT BE A GOOD IDEA TO MOVE TO A SAFER DISTANCE WHILE WE SEE WHAT THIS IS ALL ABOUT.

HAVE ALREADY MADE COURSE ADJUSTMENTS. EVERY TIME I DO, THE ENTITY CHANGES ITS TRAJECTORY TO MATCH OURS.

I BELIEVE IT'S CHOOSING A COLLISION COURSE.

OKAY, SO WE HAVE TO ASSUME IT'S A HOSTILE. WE'VE GOT TO STOP THIS U.F.O.

U.F.O.?

AN EARTH SAYING, I GUESS. STANDS FOR UNIDENTIFIED FLYING OBJECT--USUALLY REFERS TO ALIEN CREATURES.

ALIENS?

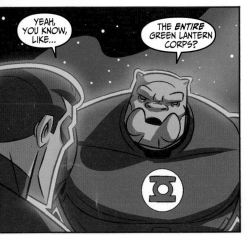

YEAH, YOU KNOW, LIKE...

THE *ENTIRE* GREEN LANTERN CORPS?

...AND THE *ENTIRE* RED LANTERN CORPS?

AND JUST ABOUT *EVERYTHING* YOU ENCOUNTER OUTSIDE OF YOUR HOME PLANET.

WELL... YEAH, WHEN YOU SAY IT THAT WAY...

ACCORDING TO YOUR DEFINITION, TO ME *YOU'RE* THE ALIEN.

YEAH, LIKE I SAID... IT'S AN EARTH SAYING.

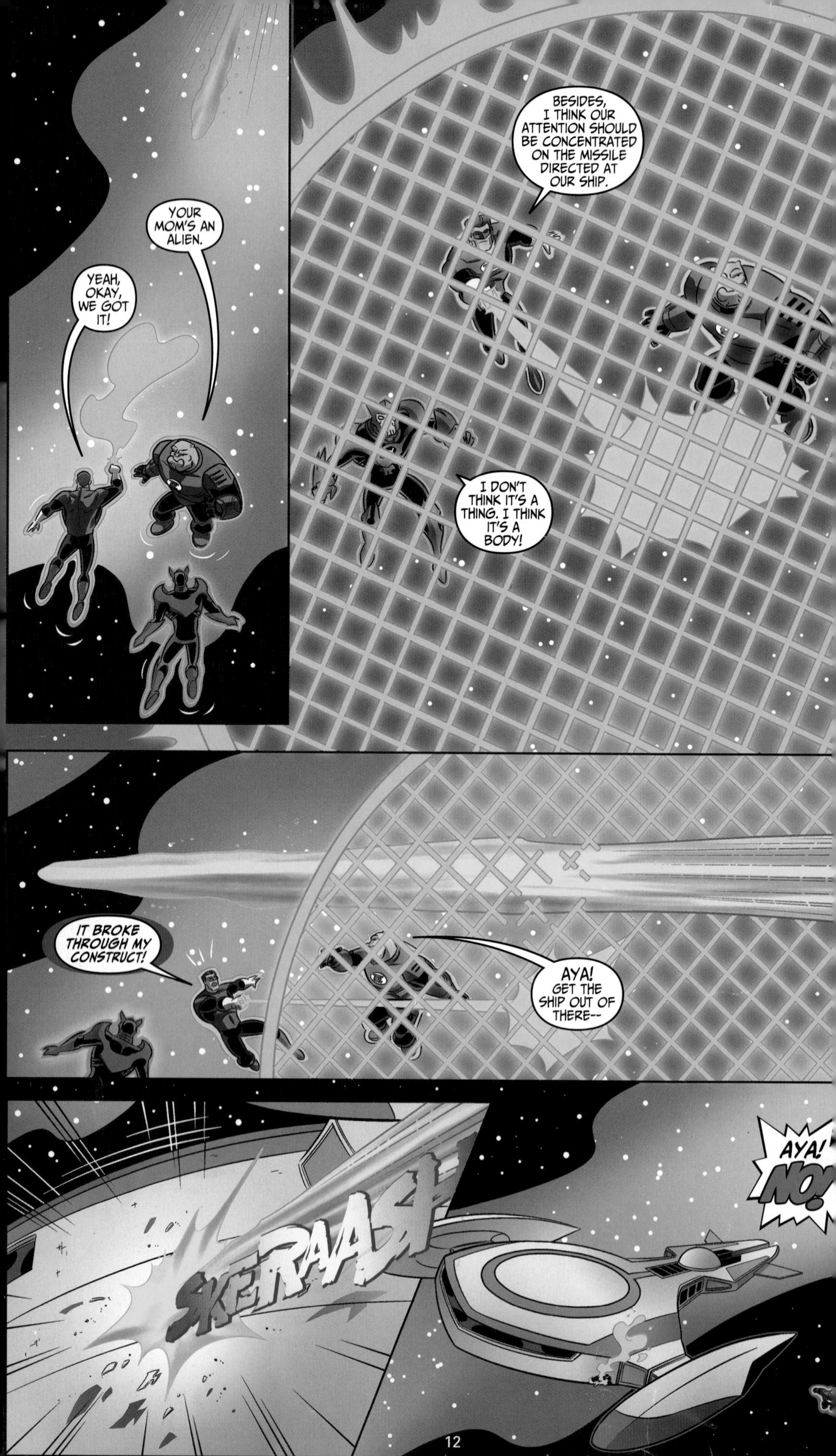

BESIDES, I THINK OUR ATTENTION SHOULD BE CONCENTRATED ON THE MISSILE DIRECTED AT OUR SHIP.
YOUR MOM'S AN ALIEN.
YEAH, OKAY, WE GOT IT!
I DON'T THINK IT'S A THING. I THINK IT'S A BODY!
IT BROKE THROUGH MY CONSTRUCT!
AYA! GET THE SHIP OUT OF THERE--
SKERAASH
AYA! NO!

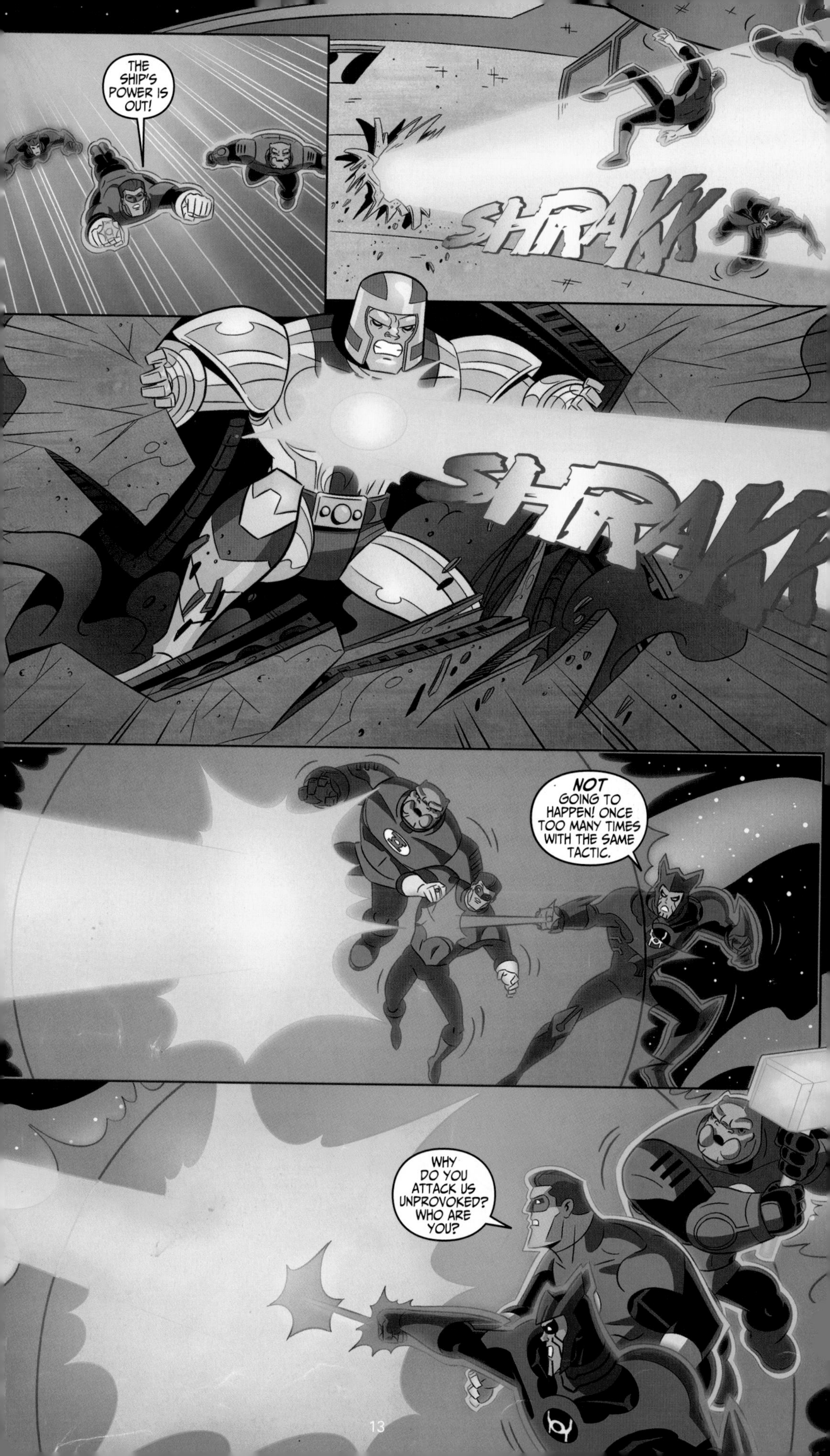
THE SHIP'S POWER IS OUT!
SHRAKK
SHRAKK
NOT GOING TO HAPPEN! ONCE TOO MANY TIMES WITH THE SAME TACTIC.
WHY DO YOU ATTACK US UNPROVOKED? WHO ARE YOU?

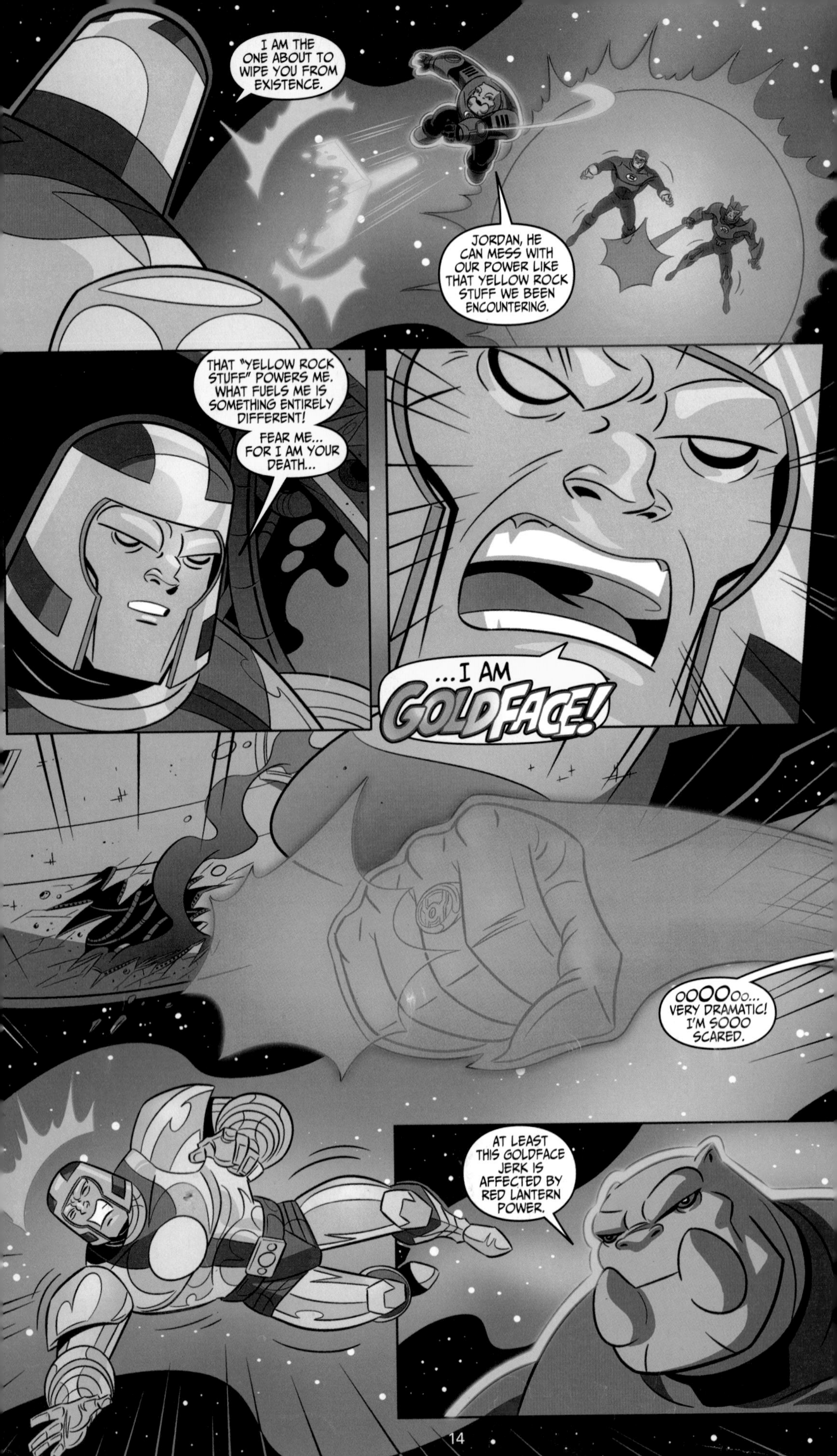
I AM THE ONE ABOUT TO WIPE YOU FROM EXISTENCE.
JORDAN, HE CAN MESS WITH OUR POWER LIKE THAT YELLOW ROCK STUFF WE BEEN ENCOUNTERING.
THAT "YELLOW ROCK STUFF" POWERS ME. WHAT FUELS ME IS SOMETHING ENTIRELY DIFFERENT!
FEAR ME... FOR I AM YOUR DEATH...
...I AM GOLDFACE!
OOOOOo... VERY DRAMATIC! I'M SOOO SCARED.
AT LEAST THIS GOLDFACE JERK IS AFFECTED BY RED LANTERN POWER.

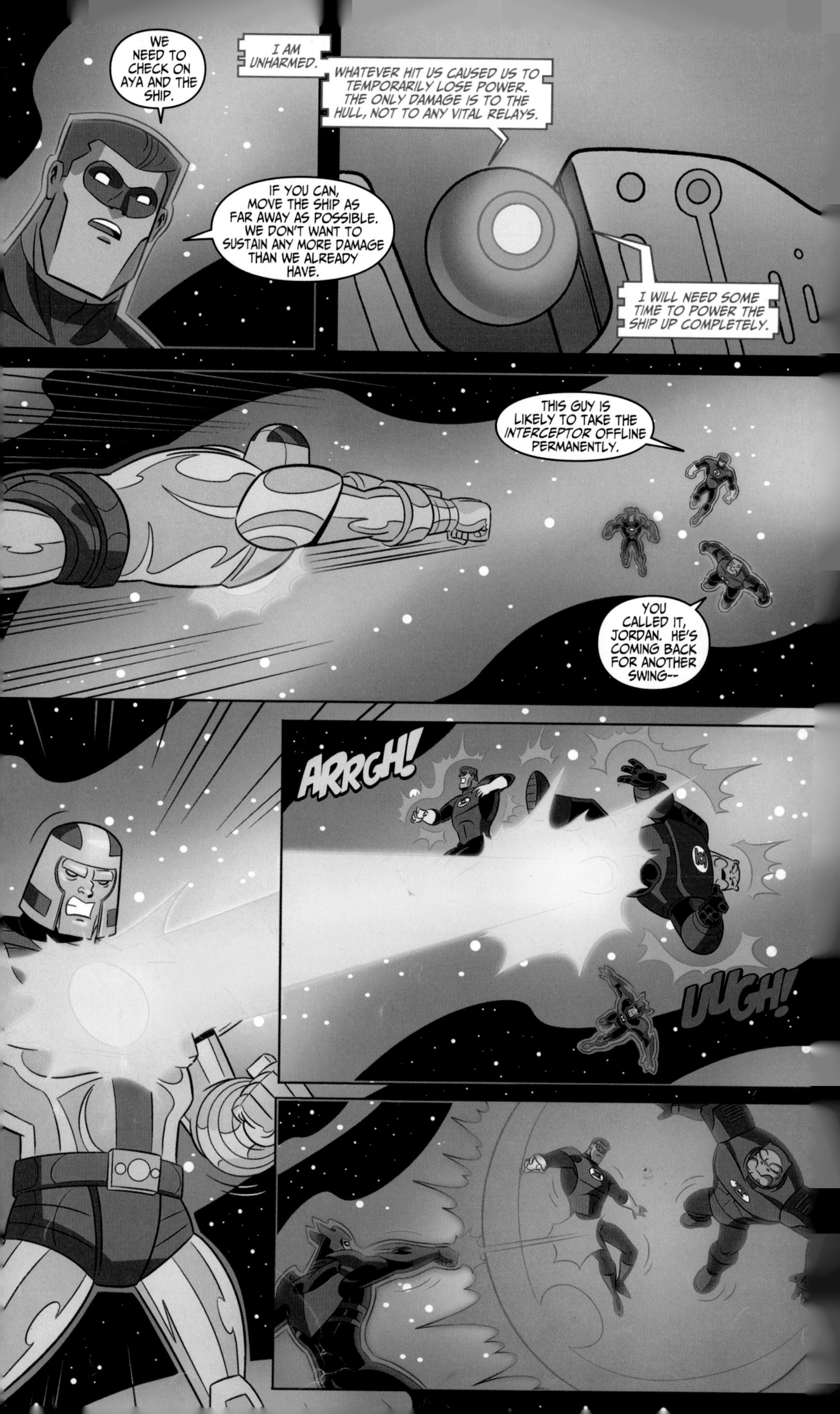
WE NEED TO CHECK ON AYA AND THE SHIP.
IF YOU CAN, MOVE THE SHIP AS FAR AWAY AS POSSIBLE. WE DON'T WANT TO SUSTAIN ANY MORE DAMAGE THAN WE ALREADY HAVE.
I AM UNHARMED.
WHATEVER HIT US CAUSED US TO TEMPORARILY LOSE POWER. THE ONLY DAMAGE IS TO THE HULL, NOT TO ANY VITAL RELAYS.
I WILL NEED SOME TIME TO POWER THE SHIP UP COMPLETELY.
THIS GUY IS LIKELY TO TAKE THE INTERCEPTOR OFFLINE PERMANENTLY.
YOU CALLED IT, JORDAN. HE'S COMING BACK FOR ANOTHER SWING--
ARRGH!
UUGH!

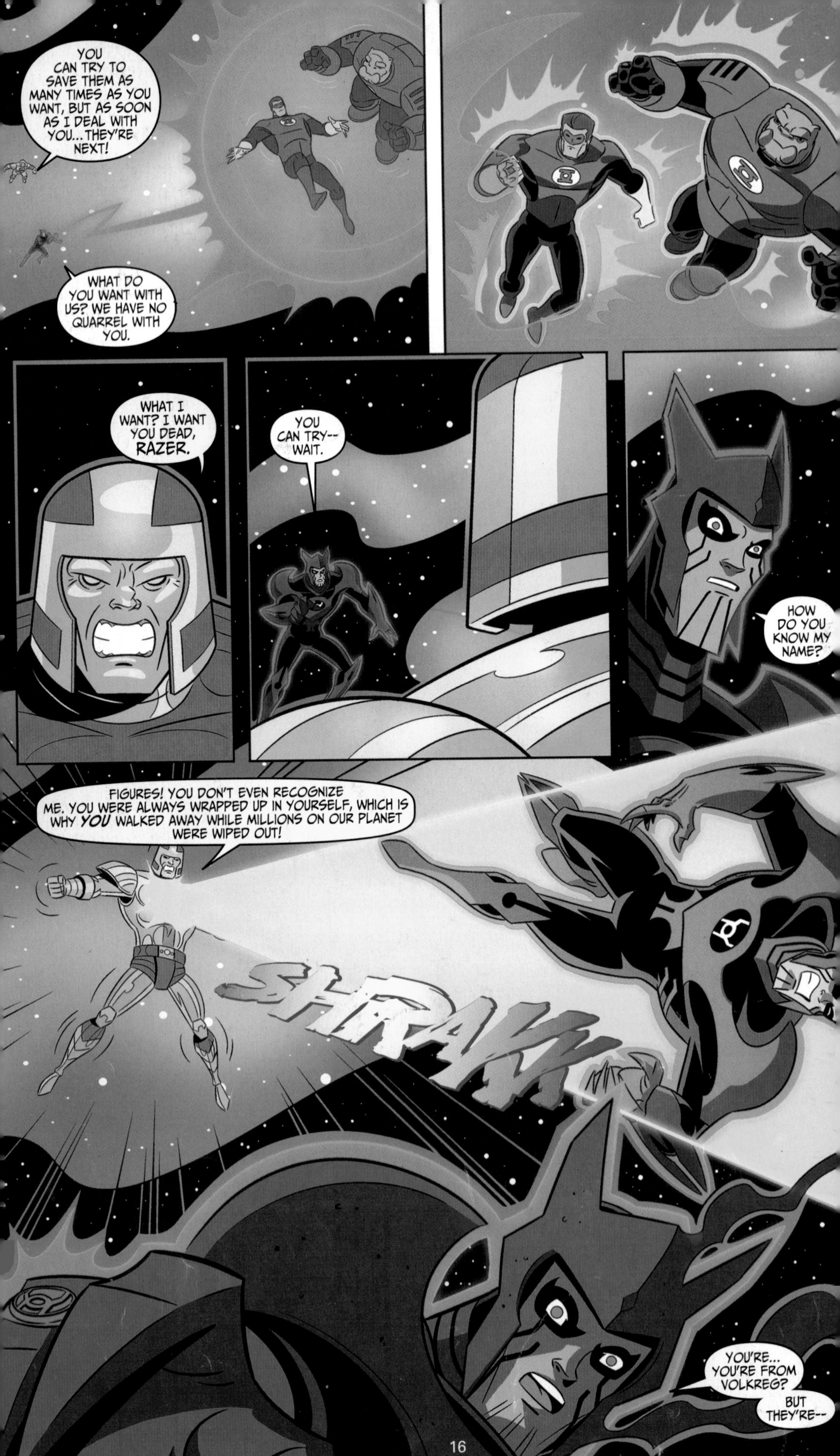
YOU CAN TRY TO SAVE THEM AS MANY TIMES AS YOU WANT, BUT AS SOON AS I DEAL WITH YOU... THEY'RE NEXT!
WHAT DO YOU WANT WITH US? WE HAVE NO QUARREL WITH YOU.
WHAT I WANT? I WANT YOU DEAD, RAZER.
YOU CAN TRY-- WAIT.
HOW DO YOU KNOW MY NAME?
FIGURES! YOU DON'T EVEN RECOGNIZE ME. YOU WERE ALWAYS WRAPPED UP IN YOURSELF, WHICH IS WHY YOU WALKED AWAY WHILE MILLIONS ON OUR PLANET WERE WIPED OUT!
SHRAK
YOU'RE... YOU'RE FROM VOLKREG?
BUT THEY'RE--

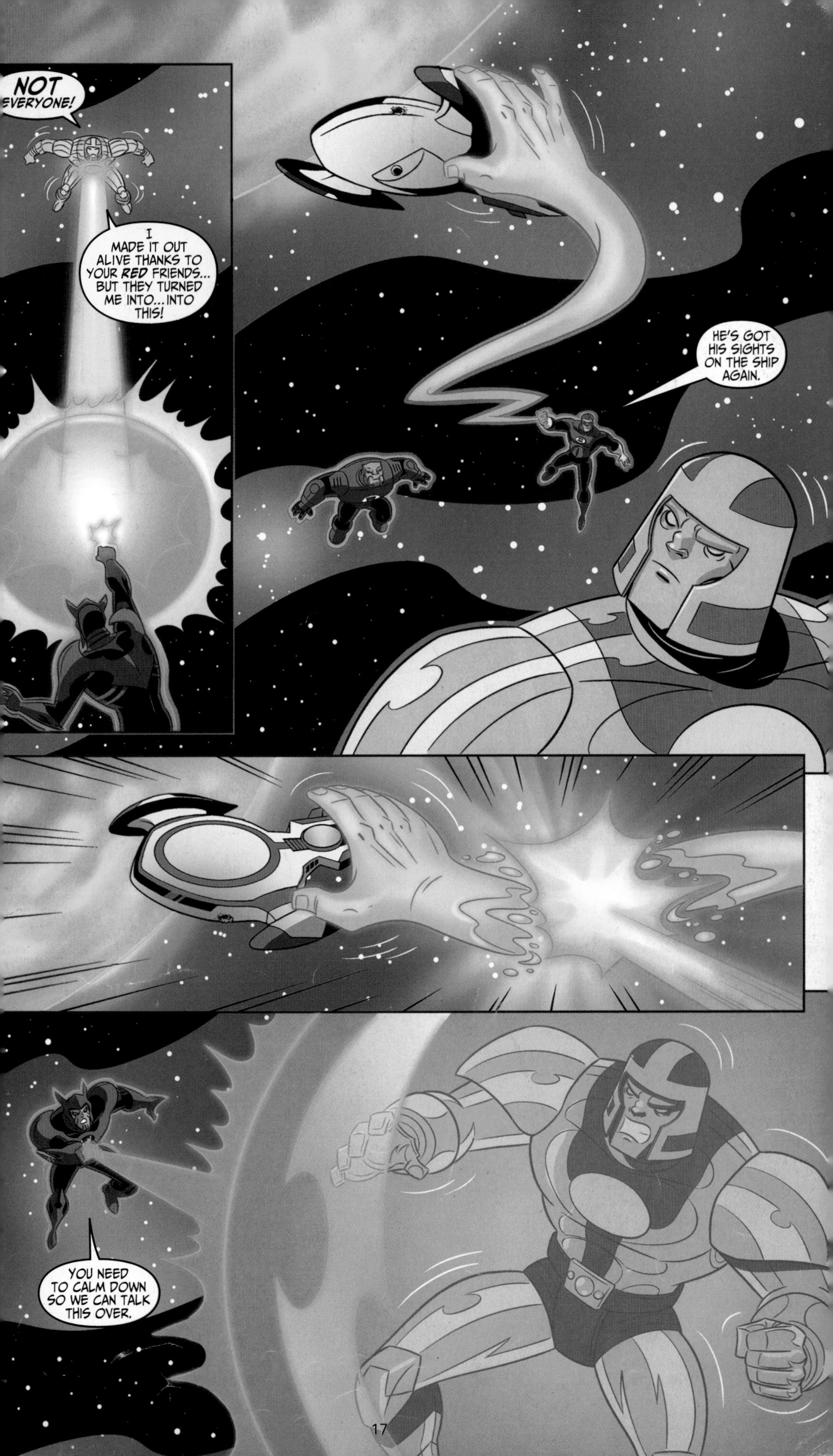
NOT EVERYONE!
I MADE IT OUT ALIVE THANKS TO YOUR RED FRIENDS... BUT THEY TURNED ME INTO...INTO THIS!
HE'S GOT HIS SIGHTS ON THE SHIP AGAIN.
YOU NEED TO CALM DOWN SO WE CAN TALK THIS OVER.

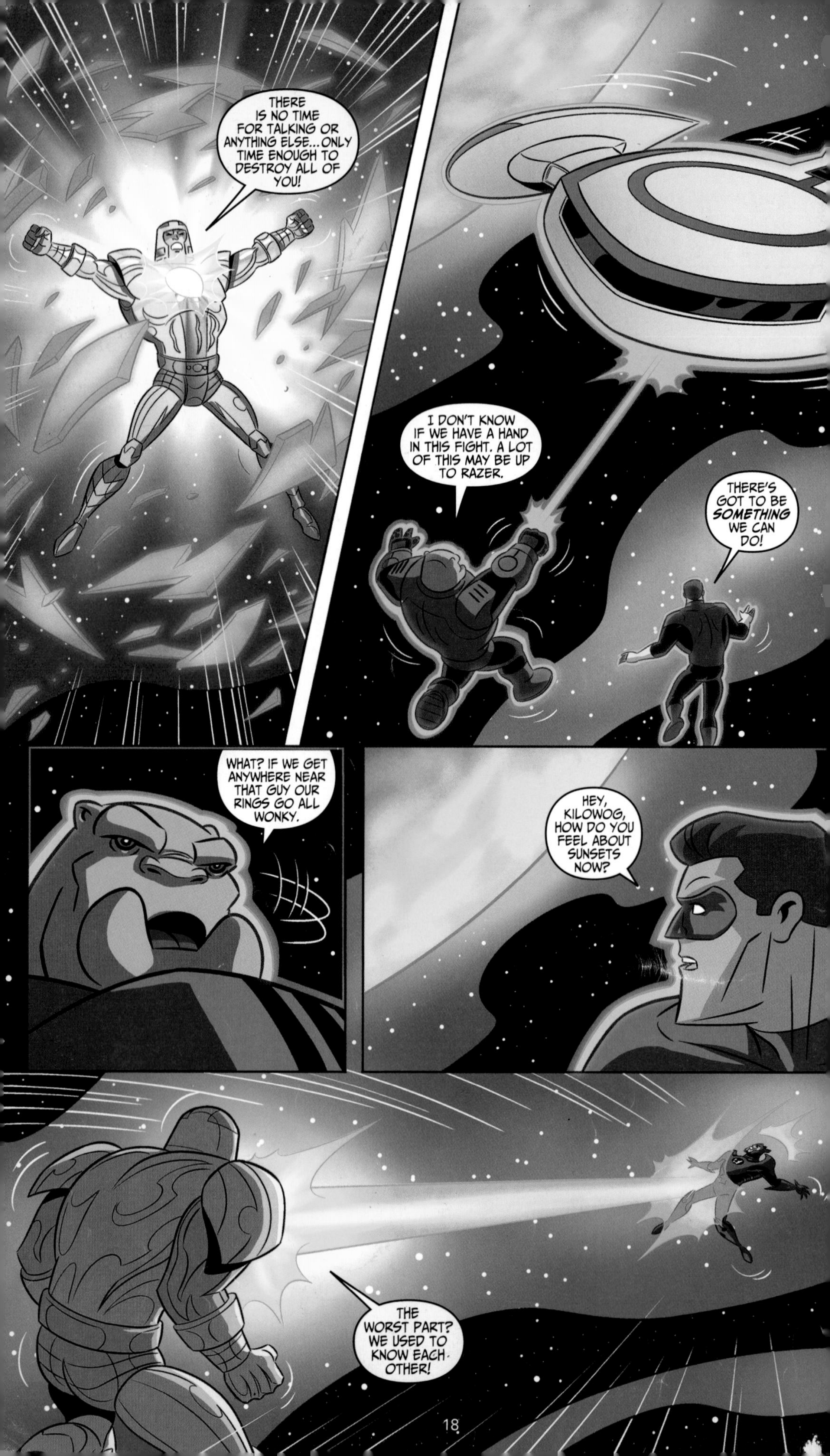

THERE IS NO TIME FOR TALKING OR ANYTHING ELSE...ONLY TIME ENOUGH TO DESTROY ALL OF YOU!
I DON'T KNOW IF WE HAVE A HAND IN THIS FIGHT. A LOT OF THIS MAY BE UP TO RAZER.
THERE'S GOT TO BE *SOMETHING* WE CAN DO!
WHAT? IF WE GET ANYWHERE NEAR THAT GUY OUR RINGS GO ALL WONKY.
HEY, KILOWOG, HOW DO YOU FEEL ABOUT SUNSETS NOW?
THE WORST PART? WE USED TO KNOW EACH OTHER!

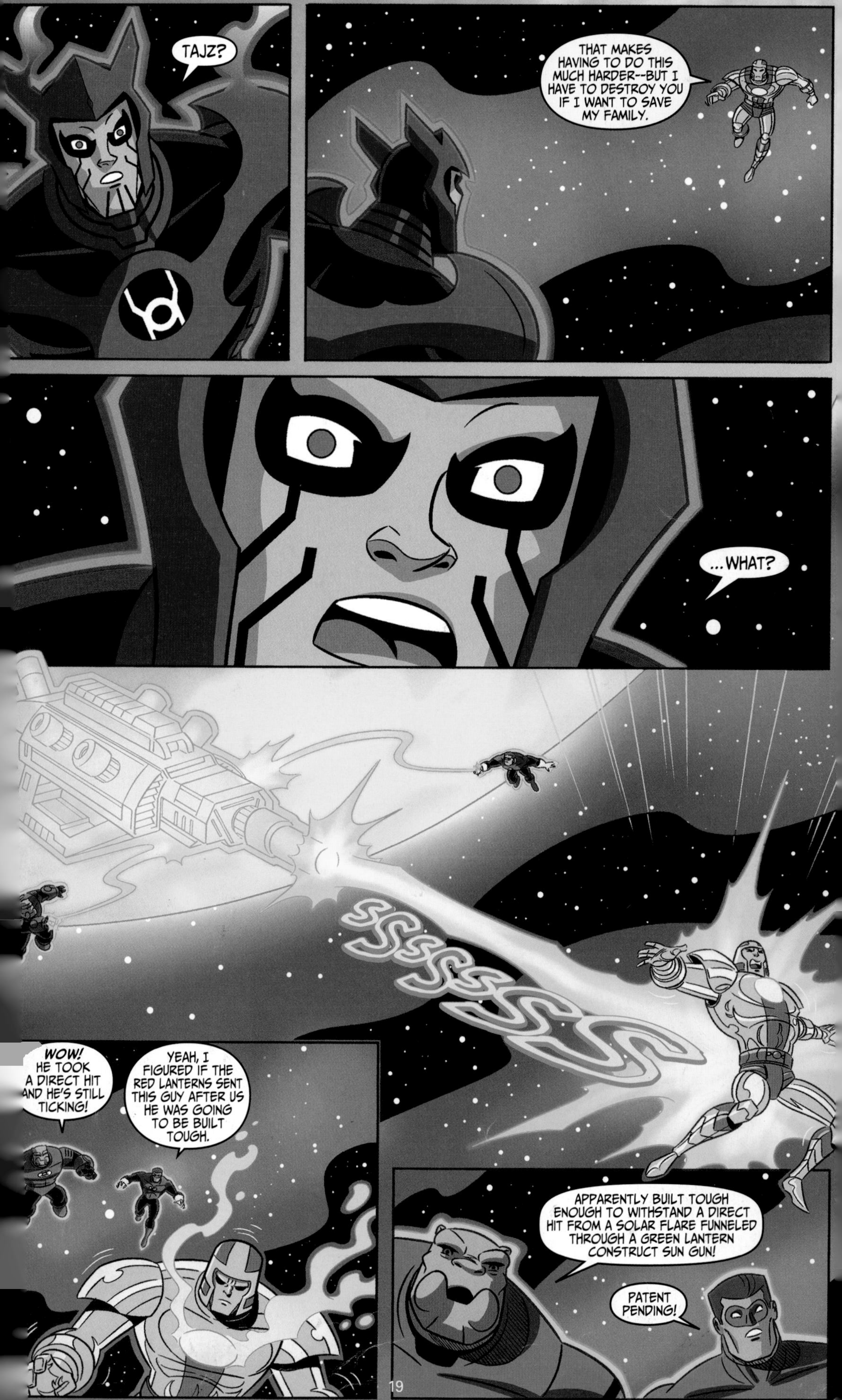
TAJZ?
THAT MAKES HAVING TO DO THIS MUCH HARDER--BUT I HAVE TO DESTROY YOU IF I WANT TO SAVE MY FAMILY.
...WHAT?
SSSSSSS
WOW! HE TOOK A DIRECT HIT AND HE'S STILL TICKING!
YEAH, I FIGURED IF THE RED LANTERNS SENT THIS GUY AFTER US HE WAS GOING TO BE BUILT TOUGH.
APPARENTLY BUILT TOUGH ENOUGH TO WITHSTAND A DIRECT HIT FROM A SOLAR FLARE FUNNELED THROUGH A GREEN LANTERN CONSTRUCT SUN GUN!
PATENT PENDING!

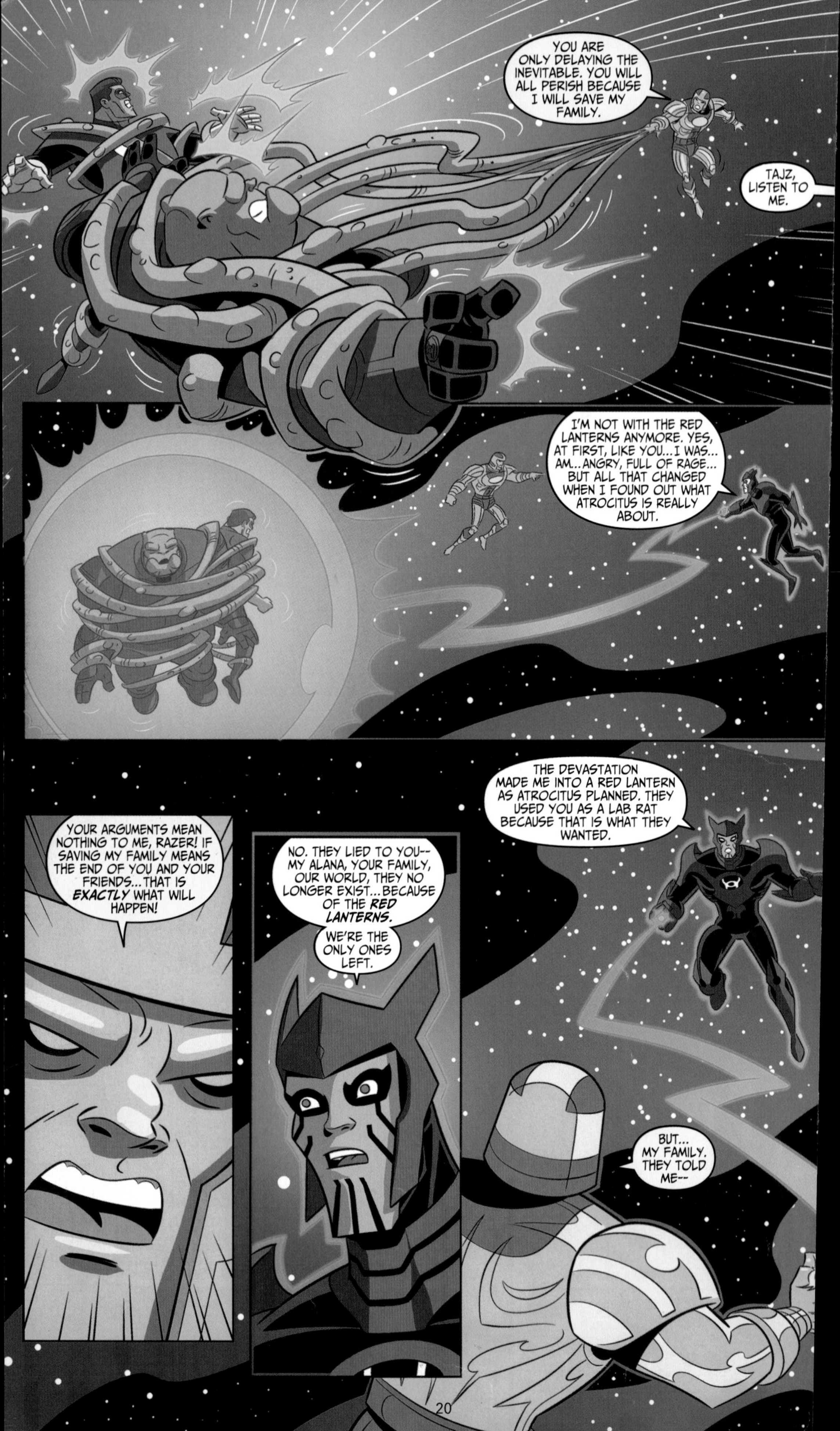

YOU ARE ONLY DELAYING THE INEVITABLE. YOU WILL ALL PERISH BECAUSE I WILL SAVE MY FAMILY.
TAJZ, LISTEN TO ME.
I'M NOT WITH THE RED LANTERNS ANYMORE. YES, AT FIRST, LIKE YOU...I WAS... AM...ANGRY, FULL OF RAGE... BUT ALL THAT CHANGED WHEN I FOUND OUT WHAT ATROCITUS IS REALLY ABOUT.
THE DEVASTATION MADE ME INTO A RED LANTERN AS ATROCITUS PLANNED. THEY USED YOU AS A LAB RAT BECAUSE THAT IS WHAT THEY WANTED.
YOUR ARGUMENTS MEAN NOTHING TO ME, RAZER! IF SAVING MY FAMILY MEANS THE END OF YOU AND YOUR FRIENDS...THAT IS ***EXACTLY*** WHAT WILL HAPPEN!
NO. THEY LIED TO YOU-- MY ALANA, YOUR FAMILY, OUR WORLD, THEY NO LONGER EXIST...BECAUSE OF THE ***RED LANTERNS.***
WE'RE THE ONLY ONES LEFT.
BUT... MY FAMILY. THEY TOLD ME--

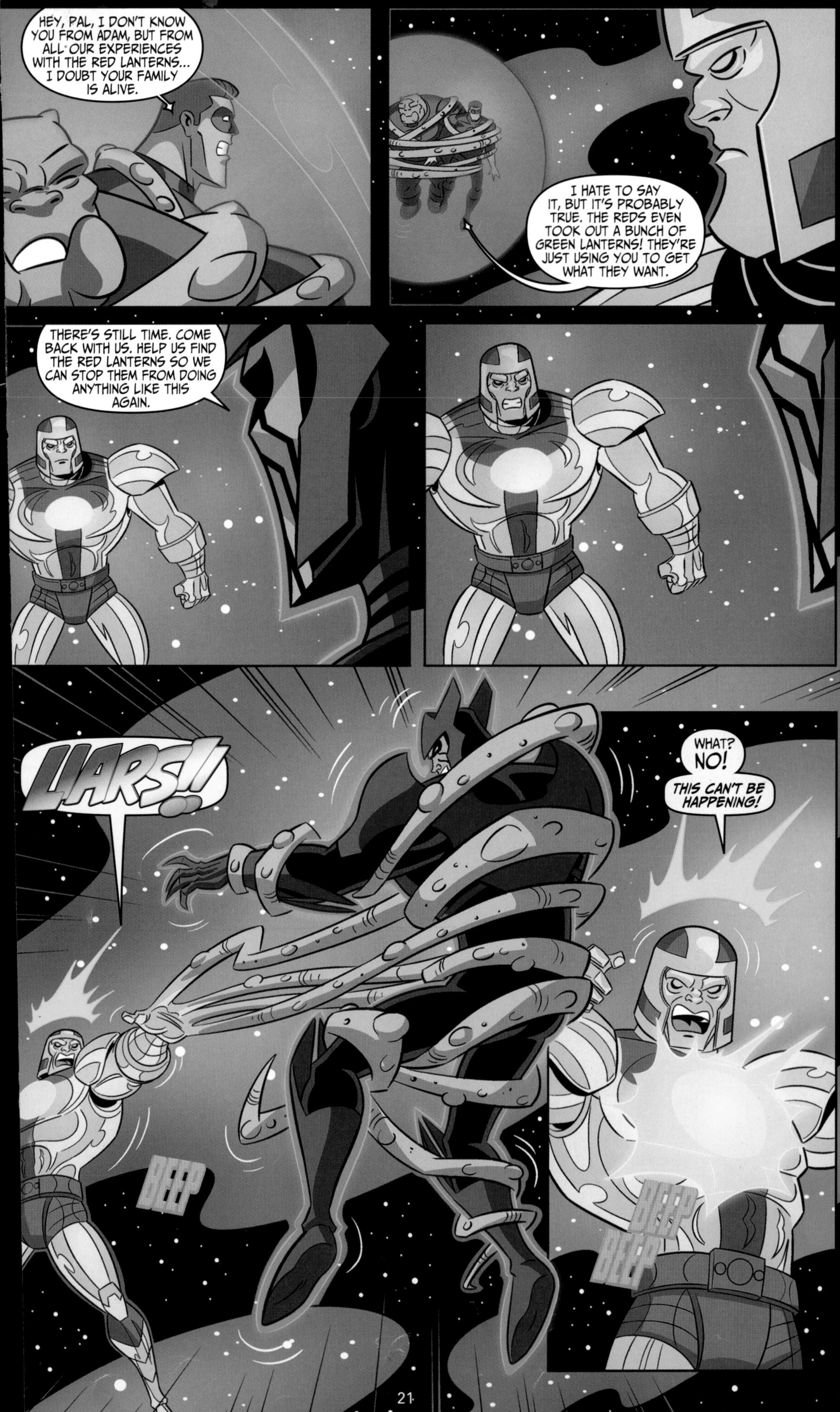
HEY, PAL, I DON'T KNOW YOU FROM ADAM, BUT FROM ALL OUR EXPERIENCES WITH THE RED LANTERNS... I DOUBT YOUR FAMILY IS ALIVE.
I HATE TO SAY IT, BUT IT'S PROBABLY TRUE. THE REDS EVEN TOOK OUT A BUNCH OF GREEN LANTERNS! THEY'RE JUST USING YOU TO GET WHAT THEY WANT.
THERE'S STILL TIME. COME BACK WITH US. HELP US FIND THE RED LANTERNS SO WE CAN STOP THEM FROM DOING ANYTHING LIKE THIS AGAIN.
LIARS!!
WHAT? NO! THIS CAN'T BE HAPPENING!
BEEP
BEEP BEEP

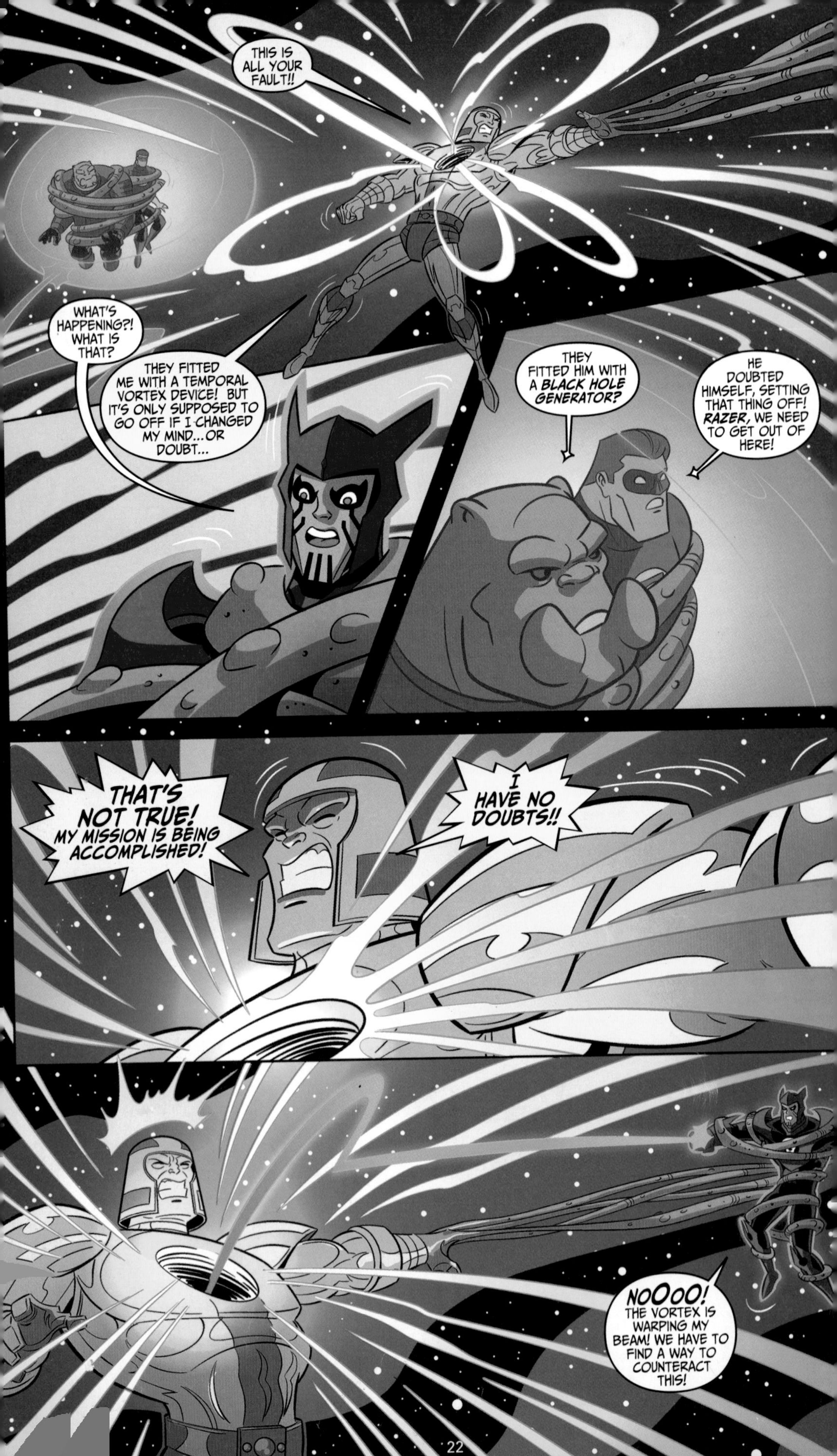

THIS IS ALL YOUR FAULT!!
WHAT'S HAPPENING?! WHAT IS THAT?
THEY FITTED ME WITH A TEMPORAL VORTEX DEVICE! BUT IT'S ONLY SUPPOSED TO GO OFF IF I CHANGED MY MIND...OR DOUBT...
THEY FITTED HIM WITH A BLACK HOLE GENERATOR?
HE DOUBTED HIMSELF, SETTING THAT THING OFF! RAZER, WE NEED TO GET OUT OF HERE!
THAT'S NOT TRUE! MY MISSION IS BEING ACCOMPLISHED!
I HAVE NO DOUBTS!!
NOOOO! THE VORTEX IS WARPING MY BEAM! WE HAVE TO FIND A WAY TO COUNTERACT THIS!

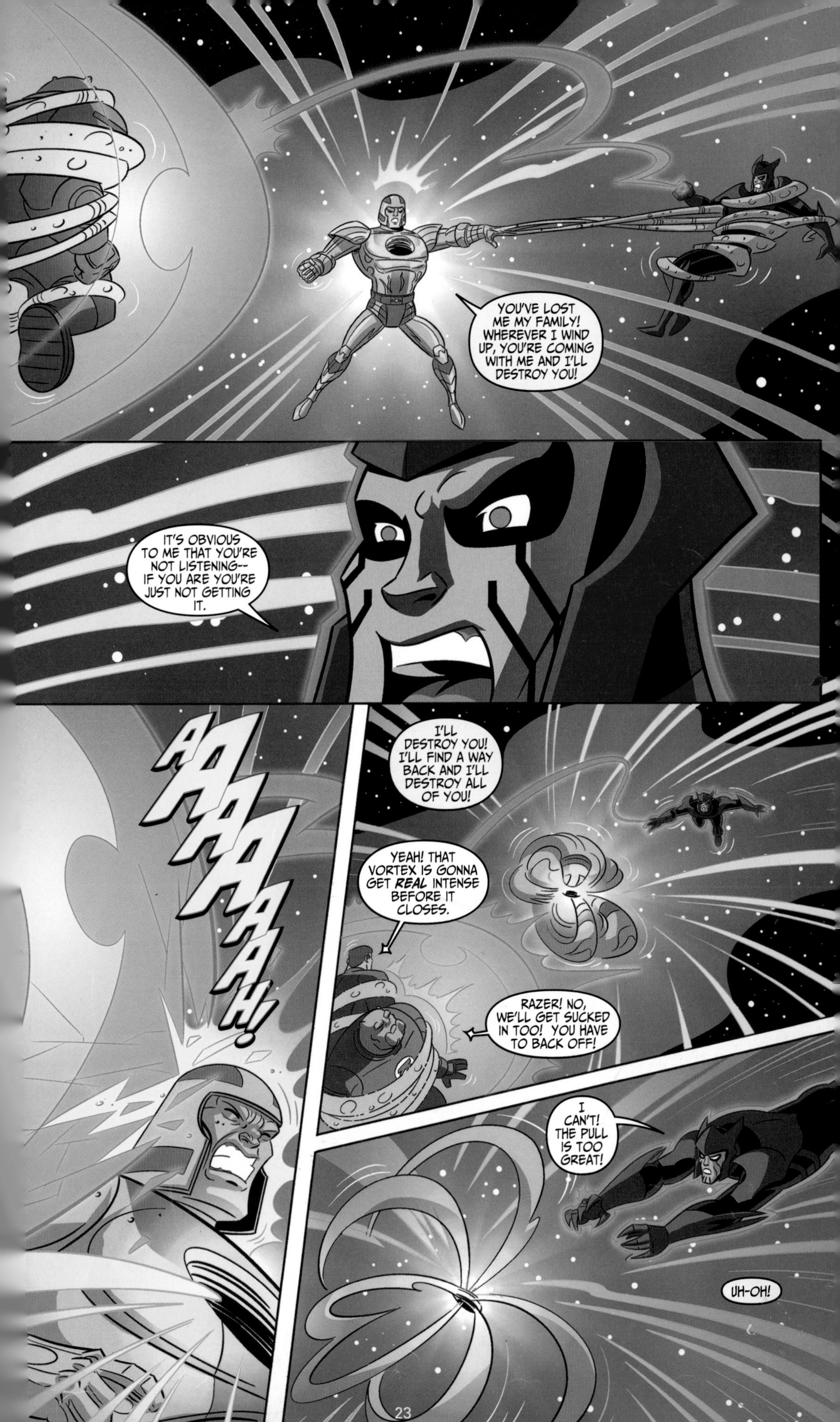

YOU'VE LOST ME MY FAMILY! WHEREVER I WIND UP, YOU'RE COMING WITH ME AND I'LL DESTROY YOU!
IT'S OBVIOUS TO ME THAT YOU'RE NOT LISTENING-- IF YOU ARE YOU'RE JUST NOT GETTING IT.
AAAAAAAH!
I'LL DESTROY YOU! I'LL FIND A WAY BACK AND I'LL DESTROY ALL OF YOU!
YEAH! THAT VORTEX IS GONNA GET REAL INTENSE BEFORE IT CLOSES.
RAZER! NO, WE'LL GET SUCKED IN TOO! YOU HAVE TO BACK OFF!
I CAN'T! THE PULL IS TOO GREAT!
UH-OH!

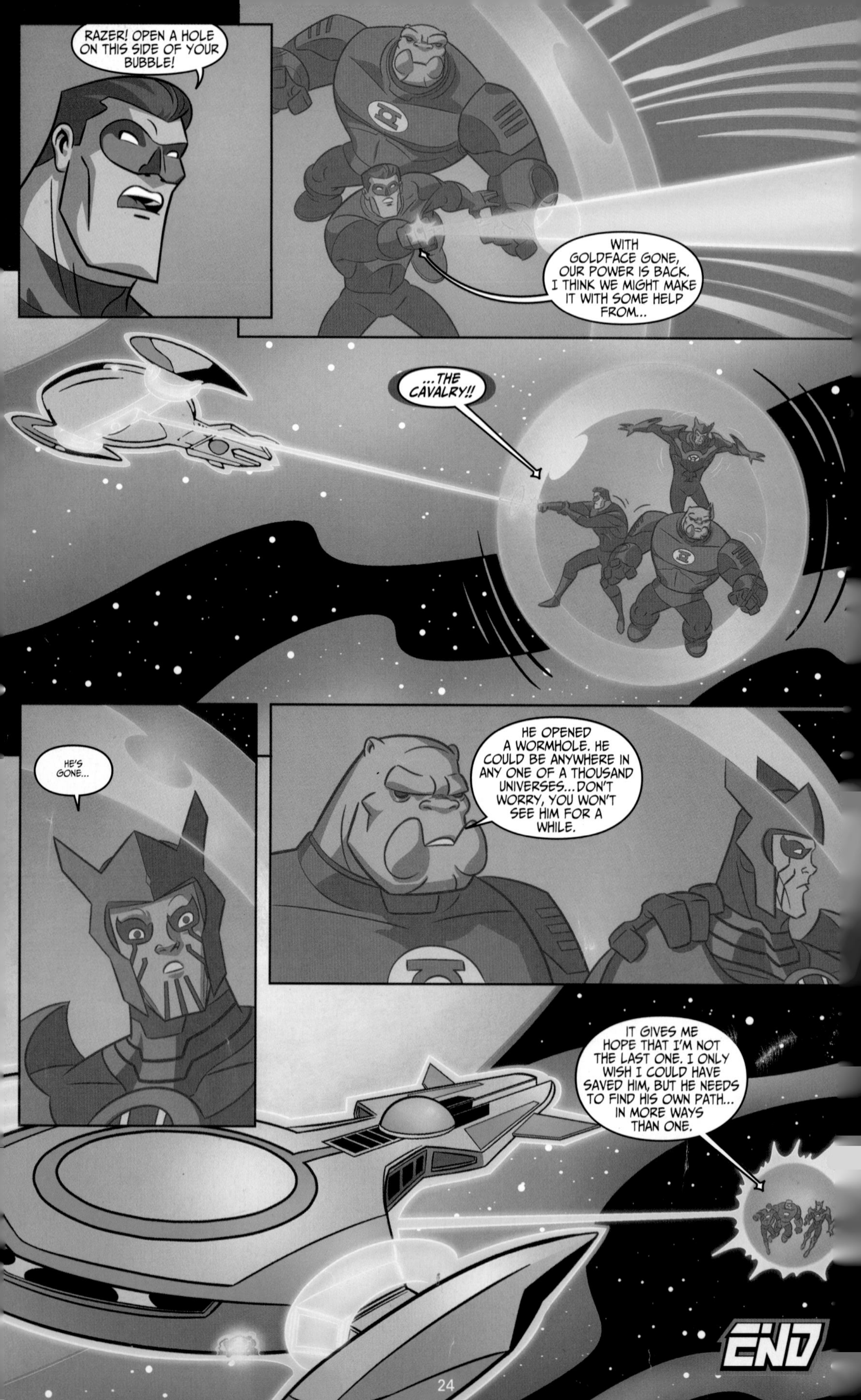
RAZER! OPEN A HOLE ON THIS SIDE OF YOUR BUBBLE!
WITH GOLDFACE GONE, OUR POWER IS BACK. I THINK WE MIGHT MAKE IT WITH SOME HELP FROM...
...THE CAVALRY!!
HE'S GONE...
HE OPENED A WORMHOLE. HE COULD BE ANYWHERE IN ANY ONE OF A THOUSAND UNIVERSES...DON'T WORRY, YOU WON'T SEE HIM FOR A WHILE.
IT GIVES ME HOPE THAT I'M NOT THE LAST ONE. I ONLY WISH I COULD HAVE SAVED HIM, BUT HE NEEDS TO FIND HIS OWN PATH... IN MORE WAYS THAN ONE.
END

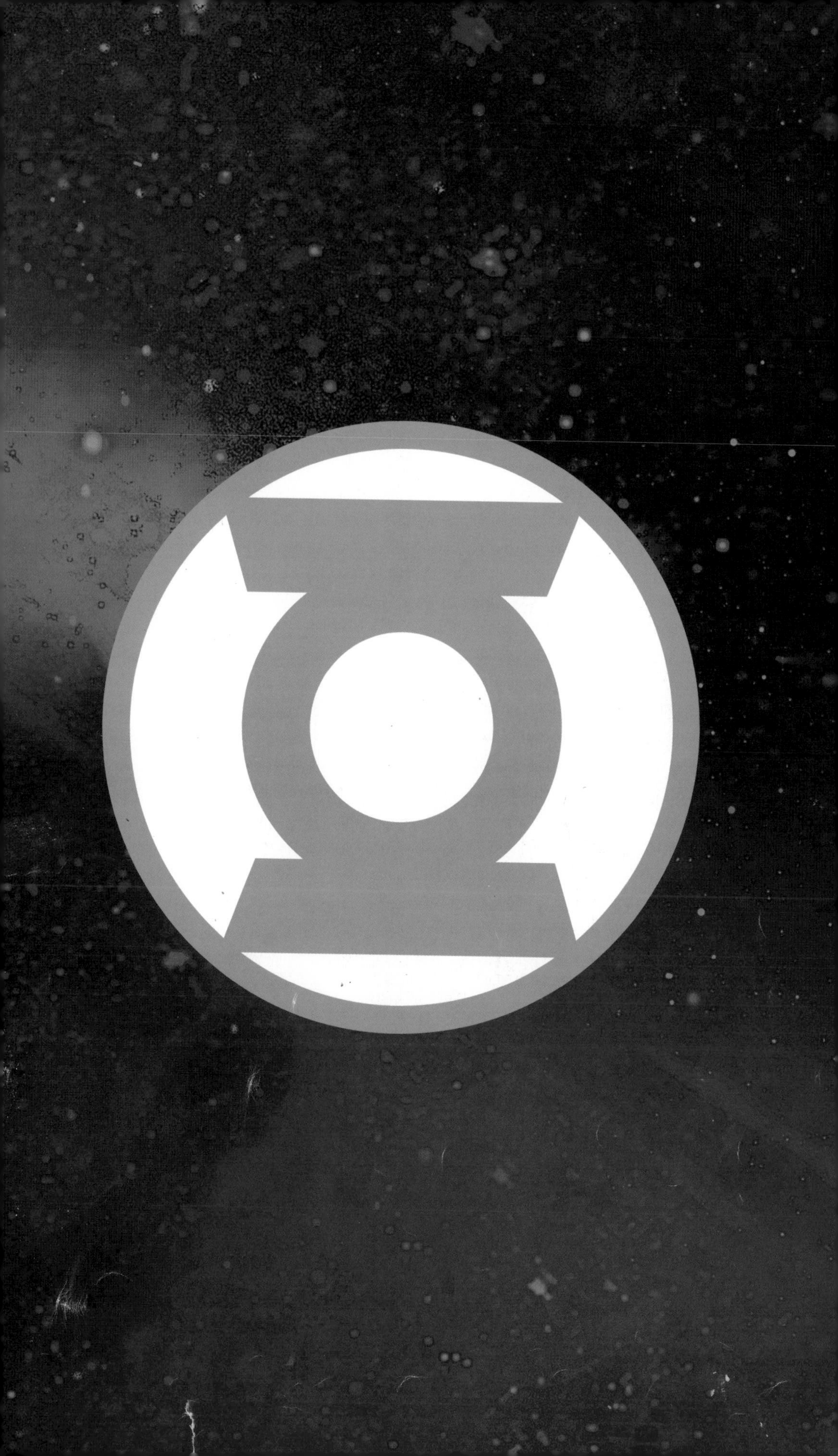

DRAW YOUR OWN HAL JORDAN, GREEN LANTERN!

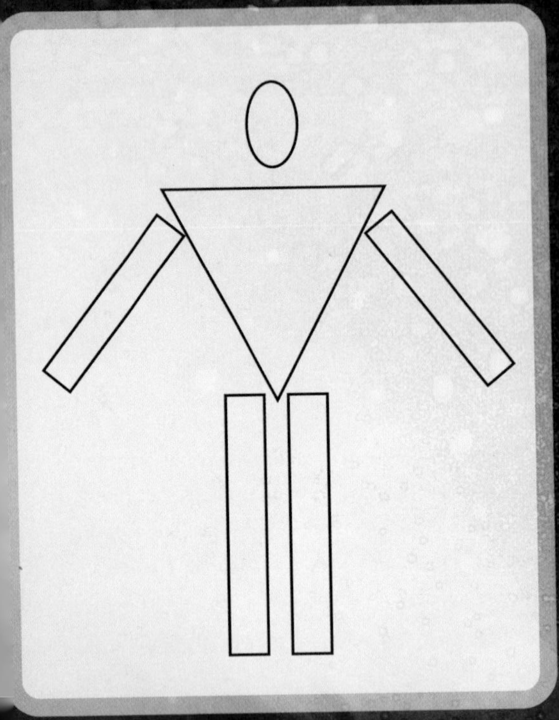

1.) Using a pencil, start with some basic shapes to build a "body."

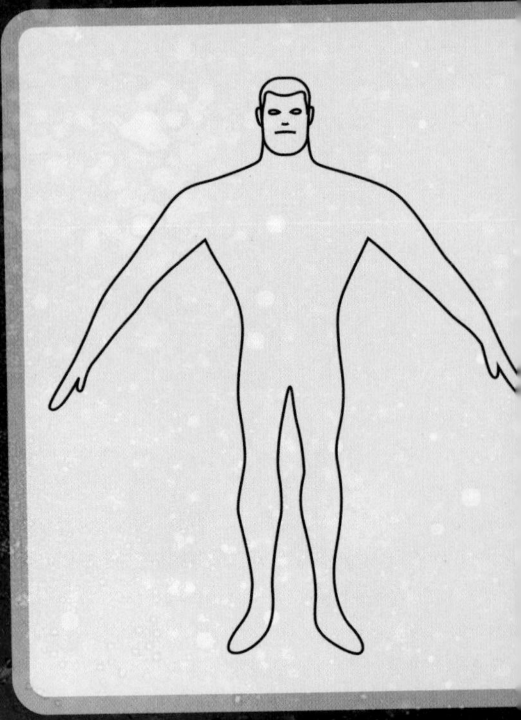

2.) Smooth your outline, and begin adding facia features.

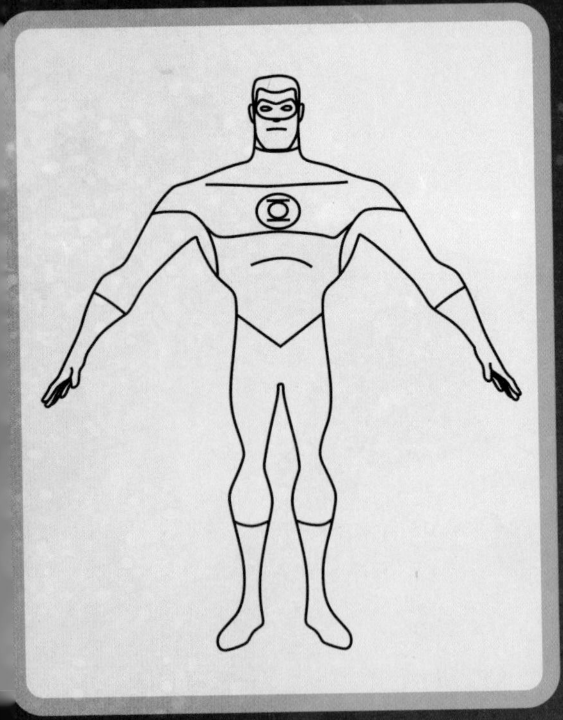

3.) Add in costume details, like Hal's mask, gloves, and Green Lantern symbol.

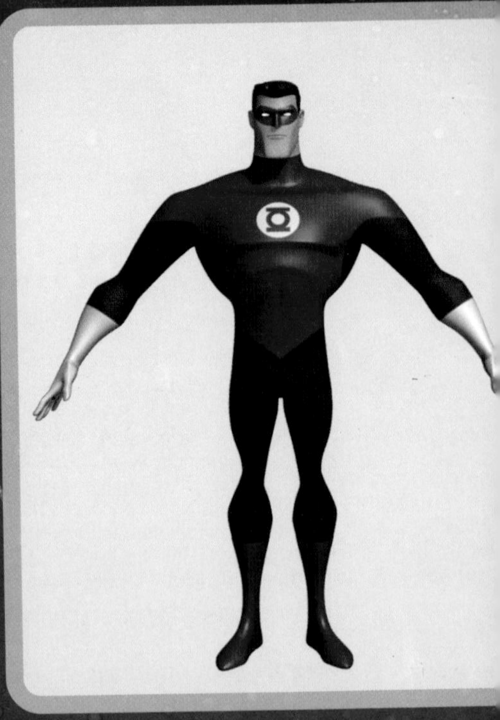

4.) Fill in the colors with crayons or markers.

CREATORS

ART BALTAZAR *writer*

Art Baltazar is a cartoonist machine from the heart of Chicago! He defines cartoons and comics not only as an art style, but as a way of life. Currently, Art is the creative force behind *The New York Times* best-selling, Eisner Award-winning, DC Comics series Tiny Titans, and the co-writer for *Billy Batson and the Magic of SHAZAM!* and co-creator of the Superman Family Adventures series. Art is living the dream! He draws comics and never has to leave the house. He lives with his lovely wife, Rose, big boy Sonny, little boy Gordon, and little girl Audrey. Right on!

FRANCO AURELIANI *writer*

Bronx, New York-born writer and artist Franco Aureliani has been drawing comics since he could hold a crayon. Currently residing in upstate New York with his wife, Ivette, and son, Nicolas, Franco spends most of his days in a Batcave-like studio where he produces DC's Tiny Titans comics. In 1995, Franco founded Blindwolf Studios, an independent art studio where he and fellow creators can create children's comics. Franco is the creator, artist, and writer of *Weirdsville*, *L'il Creeps*, and *Eagle All Star*, as well as the co-creator and writer of *Patrick the Wolf Boy*. When he's not writing and drawing, Franco also teaches high school art.

DARIO BRIZUELA *illustrator*

Dario Brizuela is a professional comic book artist. He's illustrated some of today's most popular characters, including Batman, Green Lantern, Teenage Mutant Ninja Turtles, Thor, Iron Man, and Transformers. His best-known works for DC Comics include the series DC Super Friends, Justice League Unlimited, and Batman: The Brave and the Bold.

GLOSSARY

devastation (dev-uh-STAY-shuhn) — destruction or total ruin

embellished (em-BEL-ishd) — decorated, often in an exaggerated fashion

hostile (HOSS-tuhl) — unfriendly or angry, or an enemy combatant

recognize (REK-ug-nize) — to see someone or something and know who that person or thing is

render (REN-dur) — to make or cause to become

repercussions (ree-purr-KUHSH-uhnz) — the effects or results of an action

suspicious (suh-SPISH-uhss) — if you feel suspicious, you think that something is wrong or bad

trajectory (truh-JEK-tuh-ree) — the curve described by a projectile, rocket, or something similar while in flight

vital (VYE-tuhl) — very important or essential

VISUAL QUESTIONS

1. What might be some reasons the artists chose to make Goldface's speech bubbles look the way they do?

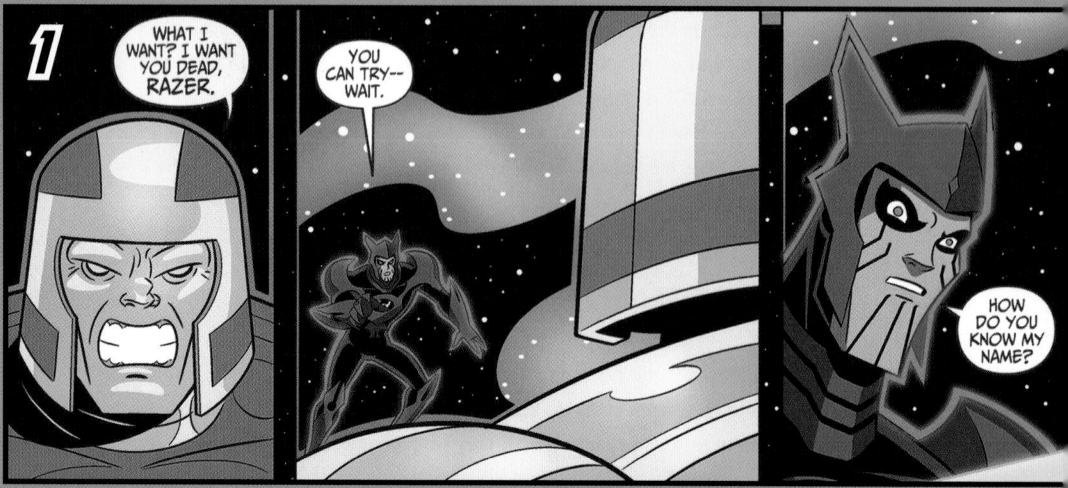

1
WHAT I WANT? I WANT YOU DEAD, RAZER.
YOU CAN TRY-- WAIT.
HOW DO YOU KNOW MY NAME?

2. In this panel, Kilowog and Hal use their powers together to channel the sun's energy into a shared weapon. What are some other panels that show lanterns working together?

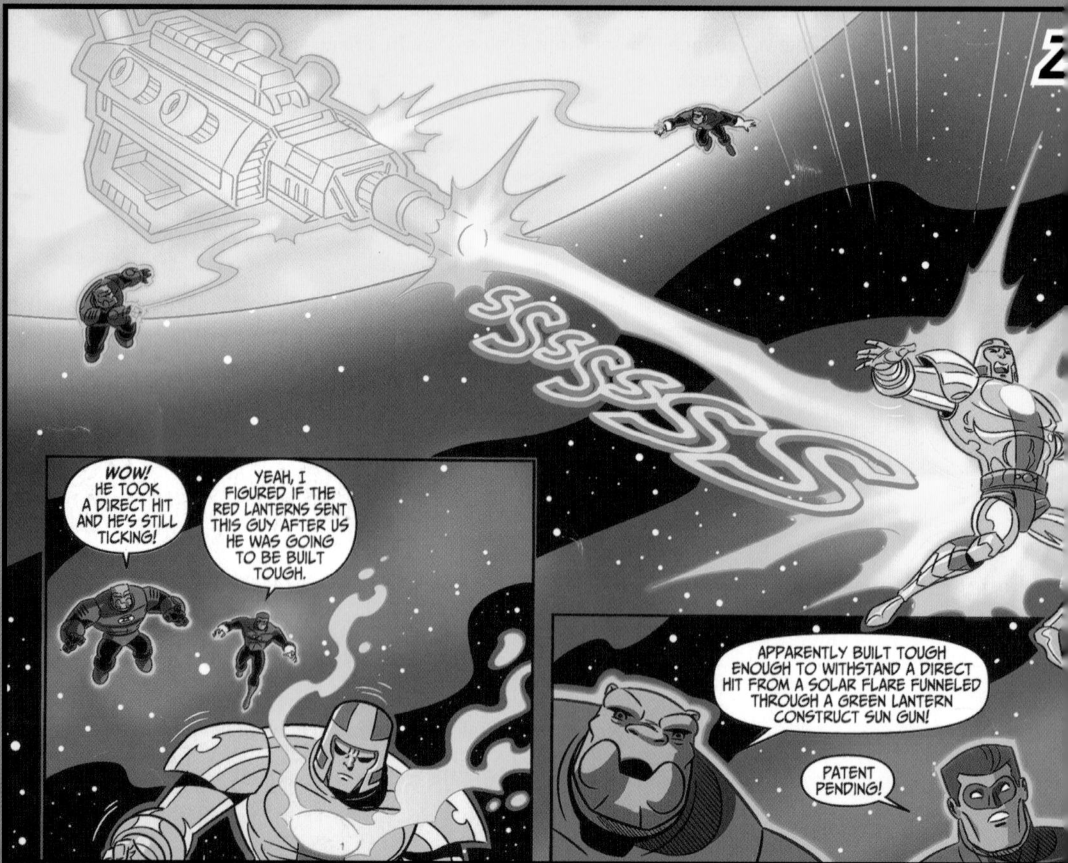

SSSSSS
WOW! HE TOOK A DIRECT HIT AND HE'S STILL TICKING!
YEAH, I FIGURED IF THE RED LANTERNS SENT THIS GUY AFTER US HE WAS GOING TO BE BUILT TOUGH.
APPARENTLY BUILT TOUGH ENOUGH TO WITHSTAND A DIRECT HIT FROM A SOLAR FLARE FUNNELED THROUGH A GREEN LANTERN CONSTRUCT SUN GUN!
PATENT PENDING!

3. What do the lines above Zilius Zox's head indicate? How do you think he feels in this panel? Why do you think he feels that way?

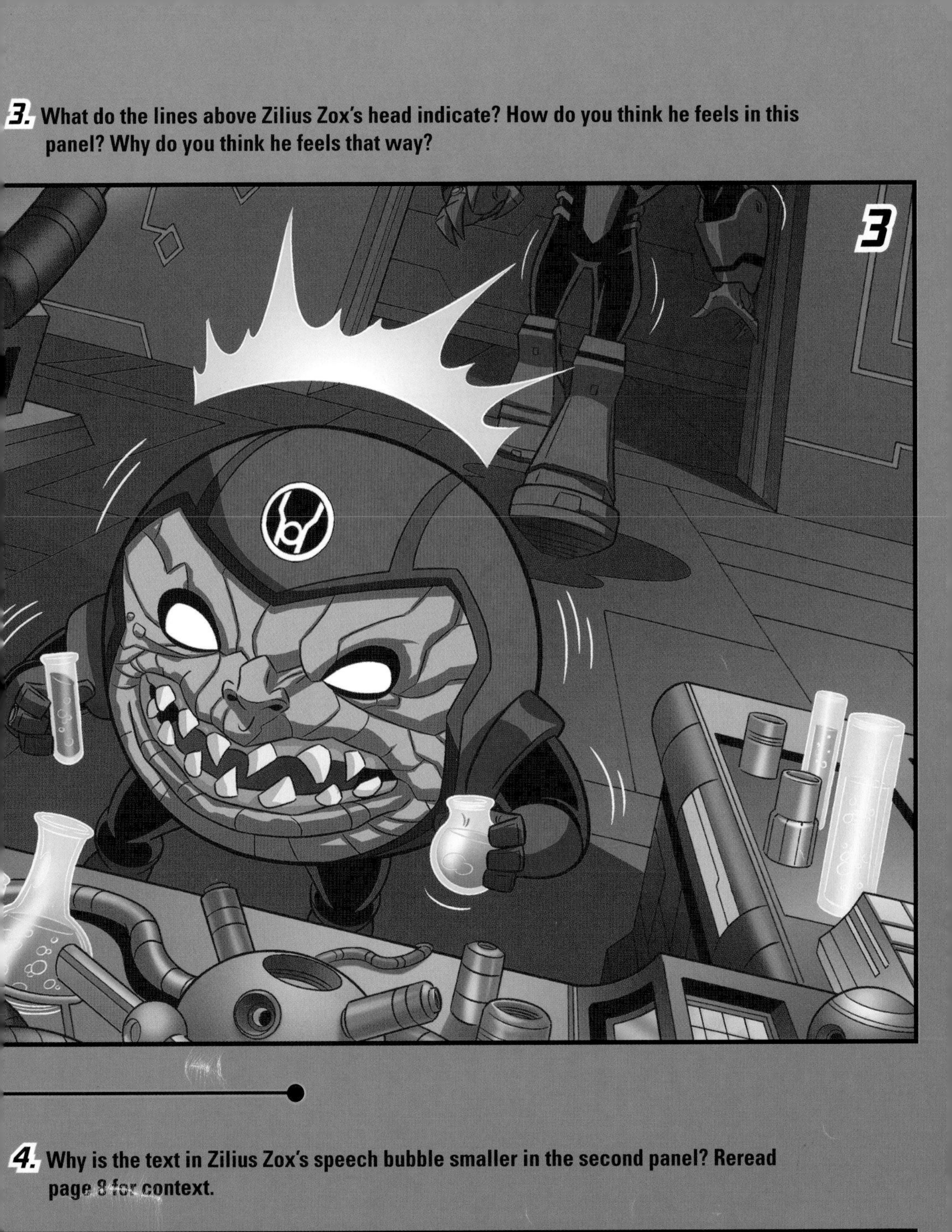
3

4. Why is the text in Zilius Zox's speech bubble smaller in the second panel? Reread page 8 for context.

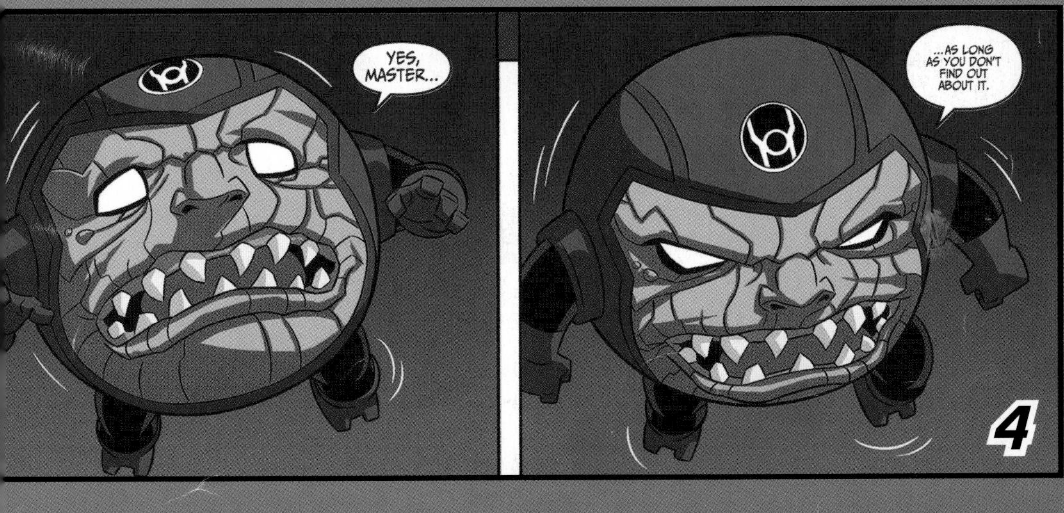
YES, MASTER...
...AS LONG AS YOU DON'T FIND OUT ABOUT IT.
4

READ THEM ALL!

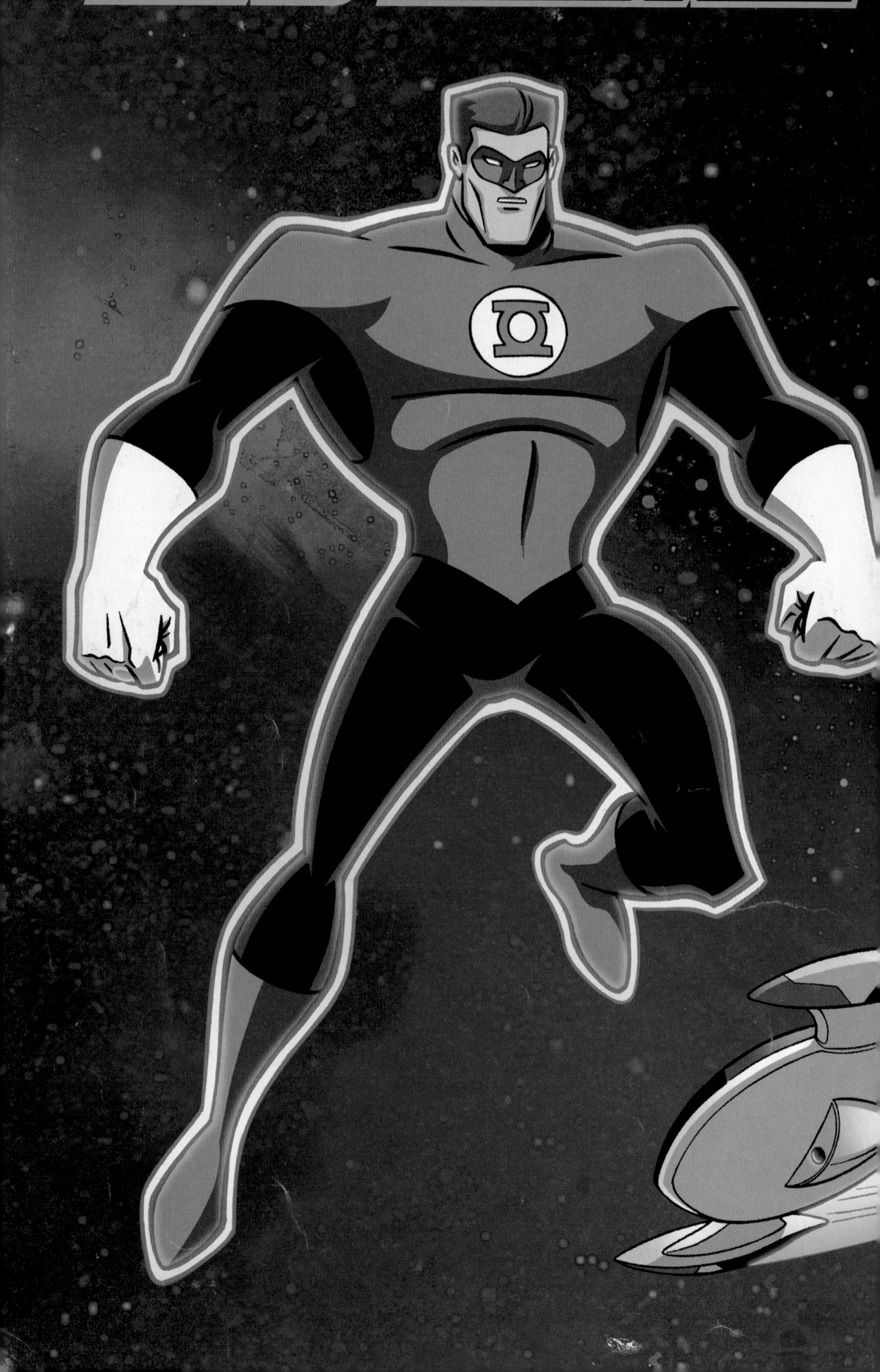

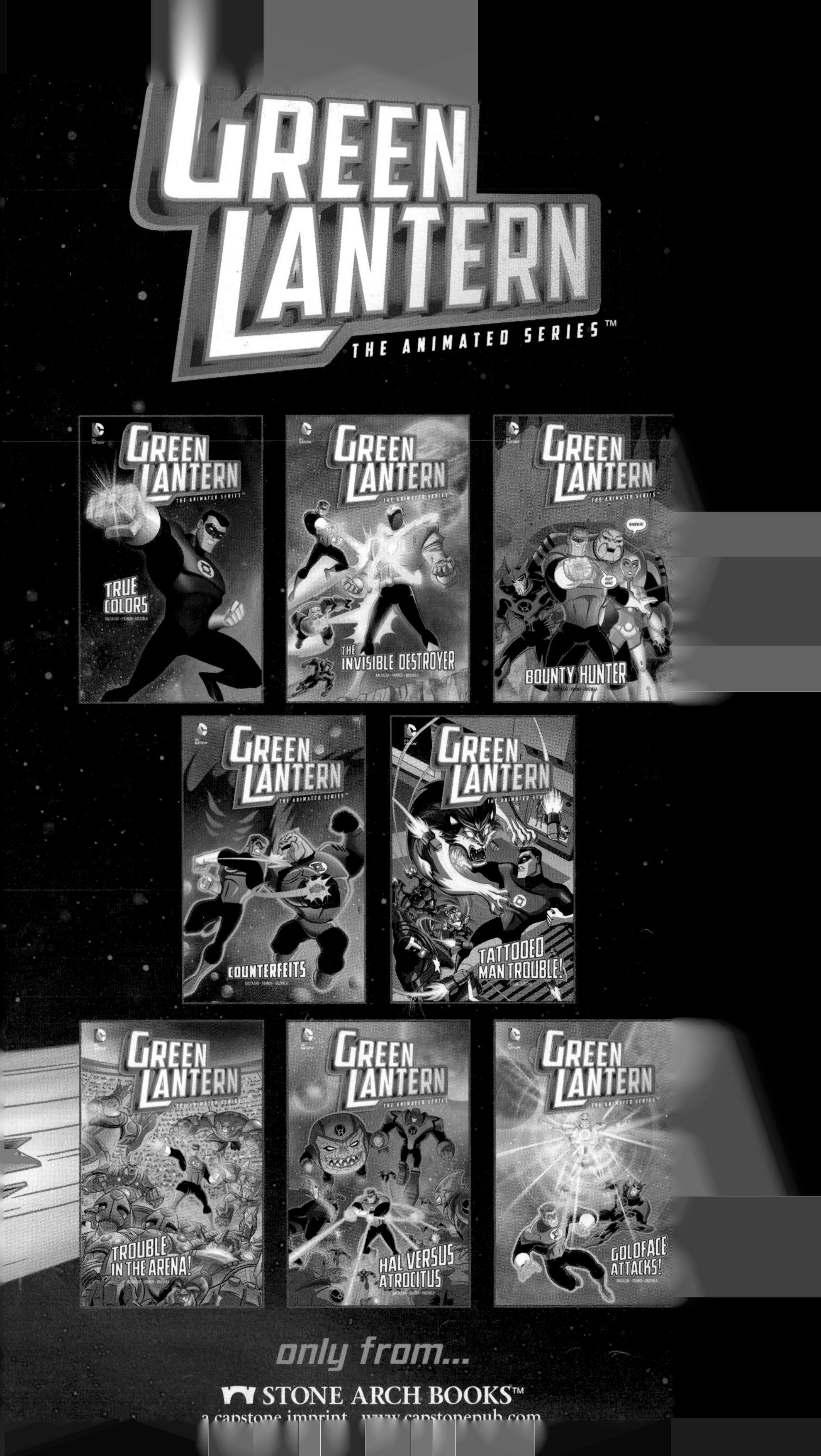
GREEN LANTERN
THE ANIMATED SERIES™
TRUE COLORS
THE INVISIBLE DESTROYER
BOUNTY HUNTER
COUNTERFEITS
TATTOOED MAN TROUBLE!
TROUBLE IN THE ARENA!
HAL VERSUS ATROCITUS
GOLDFACE ATTACKS!
only from...
STONE ARCH BOOKS™
a capstone imprint www.capstonepub.com

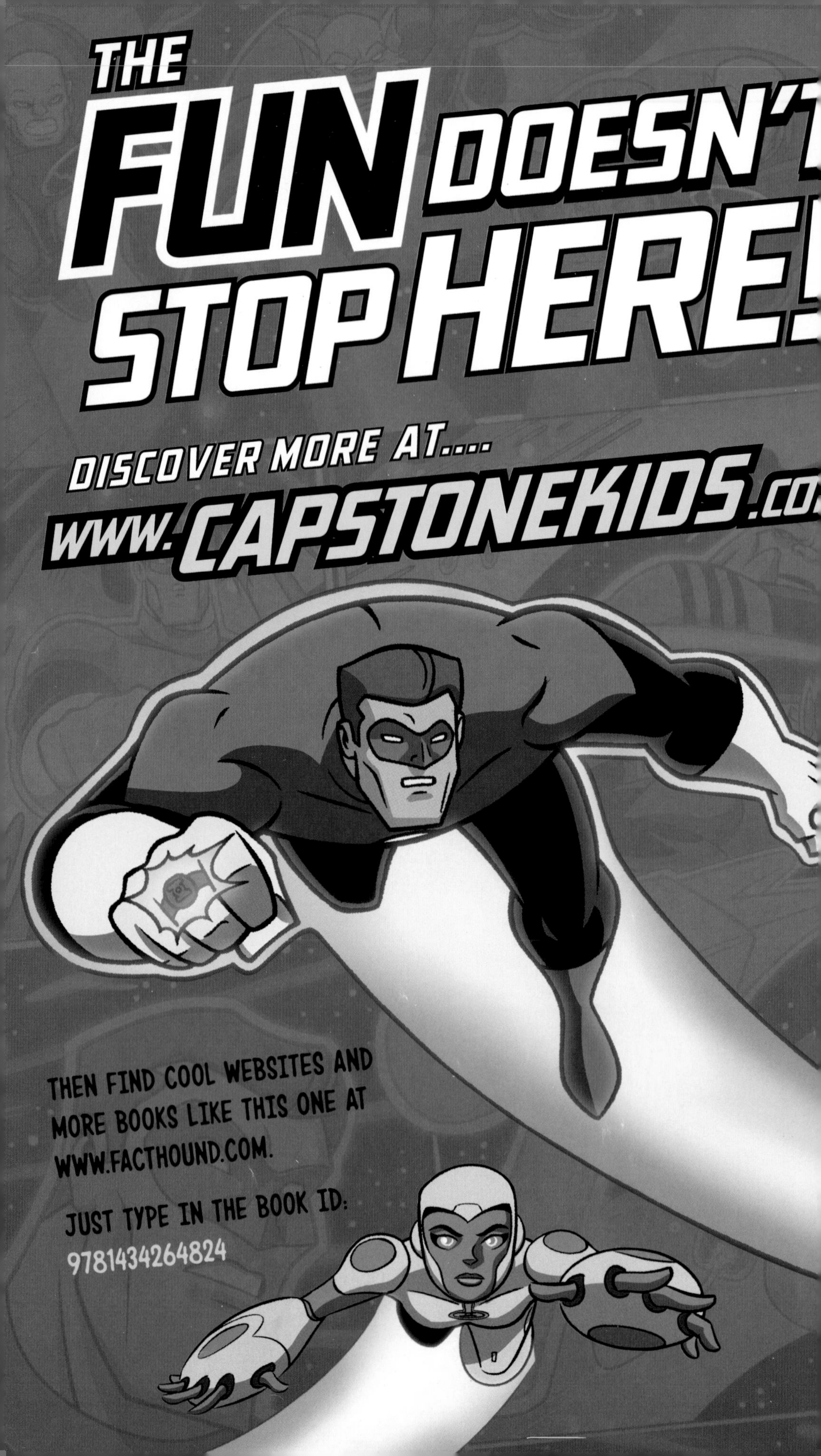
THE
FUN DOESN'T
STOP HERE!
DISCOVER MORE AT....
WWW.CAPSTONEKIDS.CO
THEN FIND COOL WEBSITES AND
MORE BOOKS LIKE THIS ONE AT
WWW.FACTHOUND.COM.
JUST TYPE IN THE BOOK ID:
9781434264824